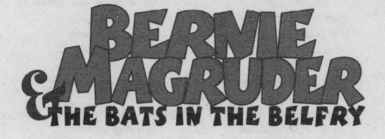

Books by Phyllis Reynolds Naylor

BERNIE MAGRUDER & THE BATS IN THE BELFRY

Phyllis Reynolds Naylor

ALADDIN PAPERBACKS

New York   London   Toronto   Sydney

This book is a work of fiction. Any references to historical events, real people, or real locales are used fictitiously. Other names, characters, places, and incidents are the product of the author's imagination, and any resemblance to actual events or locales or persons, living or dead, is entirely coincidental.

First Aladdin Paperbacks edition September 2004

Text copyright © 2003 by Phyllis Reynolds Naylor

ALADDIN PAPERBACKS
An imprint of Simon & Schuster
Children's Publishing Division
1230 Avenue of the Americas
New York, NY 10020

Also available in an Atheneum Books for Young Readers hardcover edition.
Designed by Sammy Yuen Jr.
The text of this book was set in Adobe Garamond.

Printed in the United States of America
2 4 6 8 10 9 7 5 3

The Library of Congress has cataloged the hardcover edition as follows:
Naylor, Phyllis Reynolds.
Bernie Magruder and the bats in the belfry / by Phyllis Reynolds Naylor.—1st ed.
p. cm.
Summary: Many residents of Middleburg, Indiana, are already going crazy from the ever-ringing church bells and now, after a bat is spotted in the hotel run by Bernie's family, they worry that the dangerous Indiana Aztec bat has finally arrived.
ISBN 0-689-85066-2 (hc.)
[1. Church bells—Fiction. 2. Bells—Fiction. 3. Bats—Fiction. 4. Hotels, motels, etc.—Fiction. 5. Mystery and detective stories. 6. Humorous stories.] I. Title.
PZ7.N24 Bht 2003
[Fic]—dc21   2001045817
ISBN 1-4169-0048-9 (pbk.)

To William

CONTENTS

BERNIE MAGRUDER & THE BATS IN THE BELFRY

One

A LITTLE BIT NUTS

The Bessledorf Hotel was at 600 Bessledorf Street between the bus depot and the funeral parlor. Officer Feeney said that some folks came into town on one side of the hotel and exited on the other. The Bessledorf had thirty rooms, not counting the apartment where Bernie Magruder's family lived, and Officer Feeney said that the hotel was a haven for nut cakes, as far as he was concerned.

"What do you mean? We're all crazy?" Bernie asked as he and the policeman sat across from each other in the drugstore, each enjoying a chocolate sundae.

"You and half the town of Middleburg," Feeney said. "Half the town was a little bit nuts to begin with, and the other half's headin' in that direction. And I'll tell you what's doin' the job: those blankety bells in the belfry."

As if on cue, a deep-toned bell suddenly tolled four o'clock, and immediately afterward, all the bells together played "Abide with Me," as they had been doing for the past month. A quarter past each hour, the first four notes

1

of the hymn were played; at half past, the next six notes; at three quarters past each hour, the next ten notes rang out over Middleburg, and on the hour, every hour, day and night, the bells played all forty notes of the hymn.

Bernie put his hands over his ears. "Why do they *do* that?" he asked.

"Because," said Officer Feeney, scooping out the last bit of chocolate syrup in his dish, "they ring in memory of Eleanor Scuttlefoot, who died in September. 'Abide with Me' was her favorite hymn."

"How long is this going to go on?" Bernie asked.

"Forever, I suppose, because Eleanor Scuttlefoot donated those bells, and this was part of her will."

They left the drugstore and started down the sidewalk, Feeney swinging his nightstick, when suddenly Bernie noticed a bright yellow sheet of paper with black letters tacked to a telephone pole up ahead. "What's that?" he asked, and they walked over to see.

WARNING!

A rare breed of bat, the Indiana Aztec, which migrates every seventy-five years from South America to the state of Indiana, has recently been sighted in and around Middleburg. Caution: Do not disturb this bat! The species is harmless to man unless its habitat has been invaded. Thus provoked, it will attack and its bite can be fatal. The Aztec bat is distinguishable from the common North American bat by the pale green glow coming from its nesting place. Residents beware!

"Wow!" said Bernie.

Feeney stood shaking his head. "If there's anyone left in Middleburg who *isn't* nuts because of those bells, Bernie, these bats'll finish 'em off."

"All except you?" asked Bernie.

"Why, Bernie, I can keep my cool no matter what—bats, bells, you name it," bragged the policeman. "I never met a problem yet I couldn't handle."

"Well, good luck!" said Bernie, and headed home.

When Bernie stepped inside the lobby of the Bessledorf Hotel, his mother was sitting at the registration desk working on her latest novel, *Lusty Eyelids*. His sister, Delores, was polishing her fingernails on the overstuffed couch, while the cats, Lewis and Clark, sat on each arm of the sofa, surveying the proceedings through half-closed eyes.

"The bats are coming! The bats are coming!" Bernie cried.

Lester, Bernie's younger brother, dropped the doughnut he was holding, his other hand in Salt Water's cage, removing the old newspaper. He was so startled that he left the cage door wide open, and the parrot flew about the room squawking, "Hit the deck! Hit the deck!"

"What's this?" asked Joseph, the older brother. "What are you talking about?"

"On the telephone pole outside," Bernie said. "A notice about the Indiana Aztec."

"The *what?*" his mother said. Everyone went out to see.

"Well, nobody said a word about this at the veterinary college," said Joseph, studying the warning. "And you'd think we would have been the first to know!"

"Do you suppose they're vampire bats?" said Lester. "Do they eat live people or just dead ones?"

"Oh, I wish your father was home," Mrs. Magruder said. "This *can't* be good for business."

Bernie could hear the phone ringing inside, so he ran back into the lobby and answered. It was his friend Weasel.

"Bernie, have you seen the notices posted around Middleburg?" he asked. "About the Indiana Aztec?"

"Yeah," Bernie said. "We're waiting to see what Dad has to say when he gets home."

"Man, I sure hope *I* don't get bitten," said Weasel. "I'll bet if one bit you on the finger, they'd have to cut off your arm to save you!"

"And if they bite you on the cheek, I suppose they'd have to cut off your head," said Bernie.

"If I see a bat, I'm not going to bother it at all," Weasel told him. "I'll keep my eyes straight ahead. Won't even say hello. If it crawls in my bed, I'll sleep on the floor. You sure won't find *me* disturbing its habitat."

4

It was, however, the chief subject of conversation at the dinner table that evening. Even the cats and Mixed Blessing, the Great Dane, who regularly hung around when the family was eating dinner, should some dainty morsel fall on the floor, seemed to be paying attention.

"I'm going to carry a baseball bat wherever I go and fight them off if I have to," said Lester, his mouth full of mashed potato.

"I'm going to wear a football helmet when I go to work, so they won't get tangled in my hair," said Delores.

"Oh, what a wonderful idea for a novel," said Mrs. Magruder. "My beautiful heroine will go to the window to wait for her beloved, just as a bat flies in and bites her shoulder. When her love comes by that night to serenade her, he finds her lifeless body draped over the window ledge, and . . ."

"My dear, dear family," said Mr. Magruder, glancing around the table. "Let us not look for trouble before trouble comes looking for us. Let us not fear the birds and beasts of the field till we have more information, and we certainly should not go around putting bees in people's bonnets."

"What's he talking about?" Lester asked Bernie.

"Bats, I think," Bernie answered.

"If there is anything to fear from the Indiana

Aztec, we have our very own veterinarian-to-be to protect us. Joseph will ask around at the veterinary college tomorrow, and tell us what to do," said Bernie's father. "So let's not go off half-cocked with our heads in our hands, but keep our wits about us and our muzzles loaded. I just came from a town council meeting, and I assure you that Middleburg has enough to worry about already."

"Oh, Theodore," said his wife. "Do you mean there are even worse things happening?"

"Just the usual trials and tribulations, my dear," said Mr. Magruder. "Elections are coming up in November and each candidate is talking against the other. Halloween's a few weeks away, and that's worth a worry or two. If it's not the preacher's parking space people are fussing about or the hot-dog vendor down by the library, they're arguing over the church bells going off every fifteen minutes. Half the people in Middleburg open their windows to hear the music, and half close them tight. Whatever comes, my dear, we must bite the bullet, for it never rains but it pours."

And once again, the bells began to play on the half hour. Delores got up from her chair and banged the window shut. Hard. And then, for good measure, she opened the window and banged it shut again.

Suddenly there was a frantic knocking on the door of the apartment, and Mother got up immediately to answer. There stood one of the hotel regulars, Felicity Jones, a thin young woman with large frightened eyes, who cried, "Oh, Mrs. Magruder, there's a bat in my room, and I want it removed immediately!"

Two

LOOSE LIPS

If a bat were to be found in the Bessledorf Hotel, it *would* have to be found in the room of Felicity Jones. Not in the room of old Mr. Lamkin, another of the regulars who lived at the hotel—his eyesight was probably not even keen enough to notice a bat at all. And not in the room of Mrs. Buzzwell, the last of the three regulars. If *she* found a bat she would probably knock it to the floor with her umbrella. No, it had to be Felicity Jones, who spent half her time at the window composing poems to the moon.

The Magruders had long suspected that Felicity's wealthy parents paid for her to live here at the Bessledorf to keep her occupied someplace other than at home.

"Never you fear, Felicity," said Mr. Magruder in a fatherly tone. "You sit here with the family and Joseph and I will dispatch the bat with alacrity."

"Why doesn't he speak normal?" Lester said to Bernie. "Why doesn't he just say, 'We'll go chase that bat out right now'?"

8

"I don't know; that's just the way the ball bounces, I guess," said Bernie, sounding all too much like his father.

All he could think of at that moment was going with his father and Joseph. If there was an Indiana Aztec flying about the hotel, he wanted to see it with his own eyes. If there was a creature in the Bessledorf Hotel that could kill you with a single bite, Bernie wanted to be prepared.

He knew, however, that if he got up and followed them out into the lobby, his father would tell him to go back inside the apartment, so he sat in the kitchen with his mother and Delores and Felicity and Lester, watching for a chance to sneak out, while Felicity told them how she had discovered the creature.

"I was sitting at my window," she said, "whispering a poem to the moon, and I slowly became aware of a swishing sound, like a breath in the beech trees, a breeze in the birches, a wind in the willows, a . . ."

"A tornado in the tulips," said Lester, to hurry her along.

"That's right," said Felicity. "And I said to the moon:

'Dids't thou breathe upon my cheek,
Oh, lovely globe in yonder sky?
Dids't thou speak celestial secrets
To this lonely maid so shy?'"

"For Pete's sake, what *happened*?" cried Delores.

"She's trying to tell us, Delores," said Mrs. Magruder. "She just has to tell us in her own way." And then to Felicity, she said, "Continue, my dear."

"Then I saw the fearful wings and the little beady eyes, and it flew this way"—Felicity raised her arms and swooped them to the left, knocking a flowerpot off a shelf—"and that way. . . ." She swooped her arms to the right and sent the saltshaker flying.

Mrs. Magruder got to her feet to clean up the mess, and in the resulting confusion, Bernie slipped out of the kitchen. He dashed through the lobby, then down the hall toward Felicity's room just in time to see his father disappearing inside.

Bernie slipped in after him.

"Bernie, no one asked you to tag along," said Joseph.

"There is serious work to do here," said Mr. Magruder.

"I'll be good as gold," Bernie promised. "I just want to see what an Indiana Aztec bat looks like."

"Well, I don't want you bitten and bruised," said his father. "I don't want a child of mine to be the first one devoured by these vicious vampires. Stand over there by the wall, now, and don't move a muscle."

Joseph, meanwhile, holding a butterfly net, took up a position in the middle of Felicity's room, his head swiveling from one side to the other, and Bernie held his breath, waiting for the Indiana Aztec to fly out again from wherever it was roosting.

"It's possible that it flew back outside," said Joseph, pointing to the open window.

"We have to know for sure," said his father. "I don't want that bat diving around the Bessledorf dining room, swooping over sofas in the sitting room, darting . . ."

Just then there was a faint stirring, and a small brown creature rose from a dark corner of the room and began darting this way and that, dipping and diving.

"There it is! There it is! Use the net, Joseph! Catch it quickly!" shouted Mr. Magruder.

The net swooped this way, the net swooped that. Once the bat flew so close to Bernie's face it almost tickled his nose, but Bernie didn't move. He didn't even twitch.

Suddenly the door opened and Felicity said, "Did you catch it, Mr. Magruder?" But her voice ended in a shriek, for the bat flew right over her head and out into the hall.

Theodore turned pale, but he managed to say, "Don't worry, my dear. The bat is out of your room and I suggest you keep your window closed, now that autumn is here. We will escort the little creature out the front door, and you have nothing to worry about. Nothing at all."

Nothing, of course, except Joseph running down the hall with his butterfly net, but Mr. Magruder said, "Sweet dreams, Felicity," as he and Bernie stepped out into the hall, and he closed the door behind them.

Bernie's father turned to him. "Don't breathe a word of this to anyone, my boy," he said. "Don't utter a syllable. Don't so much as hint that a bat is loose in this hotel. For loose lips sink ships, you know, and my career as manager of the Bessledorf is like a fragile boat with a single sail adrift on an unfriendly ocean of circumstance and chance."

The problem was that the bat was nowhere to be seen now. The corridor appeared empty, and unless the bat was hunkered down in a corner or along the edge of the carpet, it could only have flown into the lobby. And if that was the direction it had taken, then it could go anywhere at all—the dining room, the Magruders' apartment. It could fly into the elevator, and through any door that opened on every floor.

Just let the news get out that an Indiana Aztec had been seen in the Bessledorf Hotel, just let the news reach Mr. Fairchild, the owner, who lived in Indianapolis, and Mr. Magruder might be out of a job, meaning that the family would once again be searching for a new home.

Bernie went back to the family's apartment behind the registration desk and called his two best friends— Georgene Riley and Weasel (whose real name was Wallace Boyd).

"Trouble," he said. "Meet me on the steps of the library in ten minutes."

And ten minutes later, there they were, waiting for him at the library in the dark.

"What is it?" they asked, because Bernie always told them everything.

"Loose lips sink ships," Bernie replied.

"Huh?" said Weasel.

But Georgene understood immediately. "You're not supposed to tell a soul, right?"

Bernie nodded.

"Okay, twenty questions," she said. "Is it bad?"

"Yes," said Bernie.

"Something happened in the hotel?" asked Weasel.

"Yes," said Bernie.

"Your father lost his job," Georgene guessed.

"No."

"Delores ran off with a sailor."

"No. I said it was something *bad*," Bernie told them.

Georgene and Weasel thought for a while.

"Animal, vegetable, or mineral?" asked Georgene.

"Animal," said Bernie.

"Did something happen to Mixed Blessing?"

"No."

"Lewis and Clark? Salt Water?" asked Weasel.

"No."

"Does it have anything to do with the Indiana Aztec?" asked Georgene.

Bernie nodded miserably.

"They got in the hotel?" gasped Weasel.

Bernie held up one finger.

"One? Oh, my gosh, Bernie, does anyone know?" Georgene asked.

Now that they knew this much, it didn't seem to matter that Bernie told them the rest. "Only one person, Felicity Jones. It got in her room, but now it's escaped and it's somewhere in the hotel, and I'm not supposed to tell *any*body because no one will stay there if we're infested with bats, and we'll soon be . . ."

". . . blowing about the country like dry leaves in the wind," said Georgene and Weasel together, who had heard the Magruders say it so often they could recite it themselves.

"What are you going to do, Bernie?" asked Weasel.

"I don't know, but we've got to find it and catch it."

"I heard that the best way to get rid of a bat is to turn out all the lights and open the windows, and it will fly out all by itself," said Georgene. "That's what my grandmother used to tell me."

"Yeah, but that's how the first one got in, through an open window. What if there's a whole swarm of them heading for Middleburg, and we leave the windows open and a hundred million come in?"

"Then you could call it the Haunted Hotel, or Middleburg Caverns, and charge admission," said Weasel, who usually saw the wackier side of things.

But Bernie was worried. Finally Georgene said, "The only thing to do, Bernie, is to make the rounds of all the rooms on every floor and keep our eyes open till we find it."

"The only way we could get in every room is to help Hildegarde change the sheets," said Bernie.

"Okay. We'll come over," said Georgene. "But if anybody finds it, try to get it in a jar. If you shoo it out the window, we'll never be able to examine the thing up close, and if I'm going to be bitten by an Indiana Aztec, I want a good look at what's going to kill me."

Three

BAT WALK

"What a lovely idea!" Mrs. Magruder said at breakfast the next morning when Bernie announced that he and his friends wanted to help out.

"Bernie, my boy, it is good to see you showing some interest in this hotel. It's good to see you following in my footsteps," said his father. "Some day all this may be yours, and *you* will become manager of the Bessledorf."

"Lucky you," said Delores. "You will get to take care of stopped-up toilets and sick guests and lumpy beds and burned pot roasts."

"Delores, the repair of a toilet is as noble a job as sewing straps and pounding grommets at the parachute factory," her father chided.

"And may both jobs rest in peace," said Delores. "I would be happy never to see another grommet as long as I live."

"A job well done is noble indeed," said Theodore. "Any job worth doing is worth doing well, for everyone must pull himself up by his own bootstraps and paddle his own canoe."

"Whatever," said Bernie, and he went down the hall to the linen room at the end where the red-haired Hildegarde was stacking clean sheets on the counter.

"Hildegarde, what would you say if I told you I'd like to help out today," Bernie said.

"I'd say you were sick with the fever or here to steal soap off my cart," said Hildegarde. "Now, don't you be giving away my shampoo to the neighbors, Bernie."

"I didn't come to take anything, Hildegarde. Georgene and Weasel and I just thought you might like a little help so you can finish up early and enjoy this beautiful October day," Bernie told her as his friends appeared at the end of the hall.

"Well, that I would, but I never thought I'd see *you* with a toilet brush in your hand," she replied. "Tell you what. You go in each room ahead of me and take the sheets off the bed, the cases off the pillows, and all the towels from the bathrooms. But mind you knock on every door and call out 'Housekeeping' before you go in, and, once you're in there, don't you go touching anything that doesn't belong to you."

"We won't," Bernie promised.

Hildegarde gave him the master key to the thirty rooms of the Bessledorf, and at every door, Weasel knocked, Georgene called out, "Housekeeping," and, if no one answered or asked them to come back later, Bernie turned the key in the lock and they went inside.

"Okay, here's what we'll do," Bernie said to the others. "I'll look in all the high places a bat could be hiding, Weasel will look in all the low places, while Georgene strips the beds and tosses the towels."

"Wrong!" said Georgene. "How about if *I* look for the bat, Bernie strips the beds, and Weasel tosses the towels?"

Bernie looked a little sheepish. "Okay. Maybe all three of us should do the work and all three of us look for the Indiana Aztec while we're at it."

"That's more like it," said Georgene.

"*If* it's an Indiana Aztec," said Weasel.

So while they pulled off the sheets, they peeked under the beds. When they removed the towels from the bathrooms, they used them to swat at the light fixtures and the drapes to dislodge any bat that might be hiding there. And when they were quite sure there was no bat in the room, they went on to the next and the next.

"Boy, you sure get some weird people in your hotel, Bernie," Weasel said when they walked in a room where someone was keeping a live fish in the bathtub. He pushed his glasses back up on his nose to make sure he had seen what he thought he'd seen.

"It takes all kinds to make a world," Bernie told him, remembering something his father had said.

But weird they were, because some people kept pets and pies in their rooms, waffle irons and wickets; Rollerblades and tennis rackets; trombones and turtles. Maybe folks who came to Middleburg *were* a little nuts, as Feeney said. But as long as there were guests in the Bessledorf, they were entitled to call their rooms "home" for as long as they cared to stay, Bernie's father always told him.

Bernie, Georgene, and Weasel scanned every inch of every room they could get into. Some people would not open their doors, of course, and others answered in their bathrobes with shaving cream on their faces or their hair in curlers. When Bernie and his friends had searched seven of the ten rooms on the first floor and started on the second, Georgene wasn't so sure it was a good idea.

"Maybe this isn't so smart, Bernie," she said, leaning wearily against the wall. "You know what the signs say."

"What signs?"

"The ones on the telephone poles around Middleburg. They say that if the bat's habitat is invaded, it will attack, and its bite can be fatal. What if the bat's habitat is the top of the drapes in somebody's room, and we swat it down with a wet towel?"

"Then I guess Weasel and I will run like crazy and you can catch the bat in a mason jar," Bernie said, trying to be funny.

It took most of the day to get through the second

floor, then the third, and then to go back to the first floor and start all over again in the rooms they had missed. When they were all through, they had searched every room except for two, for those had DO NOT DISTURB signs on the doorknobs.

"So much for the Indiana Aztec," Georgene grumbled when she started home that afternoon.

"Yeah, Bernie. Next time you get an idea like this, keep it to yourself," Weasel said. But Bernie knew that they were always ready to help out, no matter what, friends through thick and thin.

At dinner that evening, Joseph said, "We talked about it today at the veterinary college, and none of my professors has ever heard of the Indiana Aztec bat. One of the instructors says that it may oxidize luciferin like a firefly, and that this is what makes the green glow. We'd love to study one if they do invade Middleburg."

"Oh, Joseph, please be careful!" cried his mother. "You have a great future ahead of you. How terrible it would be to die an early death because of a bat bite!"

"It would be terrible to die an early death no matter what," said Delores, chewing on a stalk of celery. "I don't want to die until I am a hundred years old and fall on my knitting needles or something."

"I don't want to die until I'm a fighter pilot chasing an enemy plane," said Lester.

Bernie felt like odd man out. "I don't want to die at

all," he said. "Not for a bat or a plane or a knitting needle or anything."

"My dear, dear family, let us not talk of death and dying on such a beautiful October evening as this one!" said their father, rapping his fork on the table. "The coward dies many times before his death, while the valiant faces death but once! Life is for the living, and ask not for whom the bell tolls, it tolls for . . ."

Bong, bong, bong! came the striking of the big bell in the church belfry, and immediately thereafter, the strains of "Abide with Me" resounded in the air.

"I am so sick of that song that I will abide anywhere at all that I can't hear it," Delores declared. "Why do those bells have to sound off every fifteen minutes, day and night, three hundred and sixty-five days a year? Why couldn't they just play the hymn once a day and get it over with?"

"Because Mrs. Scuttlefoot was afraid her husband might forget her after she was gone, so just before they married, sixty-five years ago, she had it written into her will that after her death, the bells would play her favorite hymn twenty-four times a day, as well as a few notes every fifteen minutes in between," Mr. Magruder explained. "She was a very wealthy woman, remember. She paid for the bells, and the church feels obliged to do as she wished."

"Oh, what a love story this would make!" Mrs.

Magruder sighed. "A man grieving for his beloved wants to remember her in song, and just when he's about to marry someone else, the church bells ring, and . . ."

"Well, *I* would never make an entire town listen to 'Abide with Me,'" said Delores. "When I am dead and gone, if *I* donate bells to Middleburg, I'll make sure my picture is on every lamppost, every telephone pole, and every tree in town. And every hour, on the hour, the bells will play 'God Save the Queen.' That's what *I'll* do for Middleburg, like it or not."

four

THE SCUTTLEFOOTS

Mrs. Magruder stayed home from church the next morning to manage the hotel, and Delores stayed home to wash her hair, but Theodore Magruder took his three sons—Joseph, Bernie, and Lester—to church because, he said, "The acorn never falls very far from the tree."

"Huh?" said Lester.

Bernie thought about that all the way to church, and when he slid in the pew beside Joseph, he asked, "What do acorns have to do with anything?"

"He means that, just as acorns stick pretty close to the trunk when they fall off an oak tree, children will usually stick pretty close to what their parents have taught them."

"Why doesn't he just say so?" said Bernie.

"Beats me," said Joseph.

It appeared to be a normal service, but at eleven o'clock exactly, the bells in the church belfry began to play "Abide with Me," and the congregation either had to wait until the hymn was over to continue with the service, or they had to sing along. The organist decided to accompany the bells on the organ, so, naturally, the congregation sang along.

And then, just before the pastor began his sermon, a man in the third pew stood up and said, "I don't know about anyone else, but I am sick to death of that hymn. I'm sick of those confounded bells going off day and night, and I, for one, would like to dismantle the beastly things, roll them down Bessledorf Street, and dump them in the river."

A gasp went through the congregation, because no one had ever talked like that before in church. Mr. Magruder looked shocked at such rudeness, but before he could even clear his throat, and before the minister could reply, a woman on the other side of the aisle stood up and said, "I agree one hundred percent. When I'm brushing my teeth in the mornings, I hear that song. When I'm driving to work, it's 'Abide with Me.' When I'm eating my lunch or doing my laundry, it's 'Abide' here, 'Abide' there. I will go stark raving mad if it doesn't stop."

People stared in shocked silence, not quite knowing what to do, but then a man at the back of the church said, "I disagree! It is one of our most beautiful hymns, and I say that Middleburg should be proud—*proud*, ladies and gentlemen—proud and honored to have such beautiful music serenade us night and day!"

"Serenade, my foot!" cried a woman in the first row. "It's driving me out of my mind, that's what it's doing!"

"Then you just don't appreciate the finer things of life," another woman admonished her. And suddenly four or five people were all speaking at once, and the minister had to rap on the pulpit for order.

"Brothers and sisters!" he intoned, and the people who were standing and shouting at each other finally sat down and closed their mouths. "We are indebted to our recently deceased member, Mrs. Eleanor Scuttlefoot, for not only providing our church with the bells in the belfry, but with our organ, our carpeting, our mahogany door, and the stained glass windows in the foyer. If it were not for the generosity of Eleanor Scuttlefoot, we would be a sorry-looking church indeed."

"He's right!" murmured a man in a side pew.

"Indeed he is," said someone else.

"Therefore, it seems the least we can do, brothers and sisters, to honor the memory of our dear departed Eleanor Scuttlefoot, is to carry out her fondest wish, to program the bells—*her* bells—to play her favorite hymn for as long as her husband, Henry Scuttlefoot, lives."

And Bernie, sitting there in his Sunday coat and Sunday pants and Sunday shoes, looked over at old Mr. Scuttlefoot, whose head was nodding sleepily in the sunshine that streamed through the window, and wondered just how much longer the man would go on living.

Possibly years and years and years. Or maybe he would just slip off quietly in his sleep. Who could tell?

"And so," the minister continued, "let us hear no more about dismantling the bells and dropping them in the river, for as long as our dear Mr. Scuttlefoot is with us, we will enjoy the music with him, the hymn that his dear departed wife loved so much."

The minister gave his sermon then, about turning the other cheek, and later, when Theodore Magruder and his sons were walking home, Lester said what the others were thinking: "Hey, Dad, if we have to listen to 'Abide with Me' as long as old Henry's alive, does that mean that we can take the bells down the day he dies?"

"Be charitable, my boy," said his father. "You're thinking only of yourself."

"But if somebody got mad enough, couldn't he just crawl up there and cut those bells down?"

"I suppose he could, my lad, but don't let that someone be you," said Theodore.

Bernie tried not to think of the Indiana Aztec and where it might roost if it came to Middleburg, or how painful its bite might be, or how long after the bite it would take somebody to die. But he didn't seem able to get away from it. The bat that had flown through the window of Felicity's room had still not been found, and no one knew whether it had gone out again or had flown into one of the other guest rooms.

At school the next day, the teacher announced that the new science project would be of current interest, because the subject was mammals, and they would start their unit with bats, since the bat was the only mammal capable of true flight.

Each student was to choose a certain kind of bat and write a report on it. As it turned out, every single student chose the Indiana Aztec, so no report was more than a few sentences long, because no one was able to find out anything at all about the species, and the library had nothing on it whatsoever.

So the teacher told them about the hammer-headed bat that navigates by sight, and the fringe-lipped bat of Central America. She talked about the Brazilian free-tailed bat, and how the flying fox bat has a wingspan as long as a large goose.

Then there was the hog-nosed bat, the funnel-eared bat, the disk-winged bat, the leaf-chinned bat, the snout-nosed bat, the wrinkle-faced bat. . . . Bernie had no idea there could be so many bats in the universe, and when his teacher told about the hairy-legged vampire bat, he could almost feel it crawling along his shoulder blades.

The teacher said that the first person to turn in at least a one-page report on the Indiana Aztec, with *authentic* information, would get an A+ no matter how many words he or she misspelled. But Bernie decided that if even the veterinary college didn't have anything about the Indiana Aztec in its library, there wasn't much hope for him.

That evening Bernie took Mixed Blessing for a walk, and when he came back inside the lobby, he stepped into the middle of an argument at the registration desk. In fact, Felicity Jones and Mrs. Buzzwell and old Mr. Lamkin had stopped their game of canasta at a corner table and were watching what was going on.

A man of about thirty was arguing with Delores, who sat plucking her eyebrows with one hand and holding a small mirror in the other.

"When I put a DO NOT DISTURB sign on my door, that's exactly what I mean," the man was saying. "No maids, no workmen, no manager, no nothing. Is that clear?"

Delores put down the tweezers. "It is clear to me that you will have no clean sheets, no fresh towels, no more shampoo or soap or toilet paper," she said.

"If that's the way I want it, then that's my business," the man told her.

"It is also clear," said Delores, "that you may, in fact, begin to smell."

Mr. Magruder came upon the scene just then, and when Delores explained that the man in 107 was a slob, Mr. Magruder immediately silenced his daughter with a look.

"You are one hundred percent right, sir," he said. "A man's home is his castle, and in my hotel, each room is the customer's home. What's one unmade bed in the scheme of things, eh? What's one wet towel? We shall not enter your room until you give your permission, sir, and the DO NOT DISTURB sign on the door will be your sentry."

When the man had gone back down the hall, Theodore said to his daughter, "The customer is always right, Delores, and if you speak like that again, I shall lose my job, and we will soon be . . ."

Delores rolled her eyes, and she and Bernie recited the rest together: ". . . blowing about the country like dry leaves in the wind."

When Mr. Magruder went back to the apartment, however, Delores said to Bernie, "That man's a nut cake if I ever saw one."

"Who? Dad?" asked Bernie.

"No. The guy in 107. Every night he goes for a walk at the same time. Every night he comes home a few hours later. He never lets us change his sheets or towels, and he pays by the week. He'll end up staying here and becoming a regular, just like Felicity Jones, I'll bet. Then we'll have *four* nut cakes living here, counting Lamkin and Buzzwell."

"Then Officer Feeney was right," said Bernie.

"About what?"

"He said this hotel was a haven for nut cakes."

"Feeney doesn't know his ear from his elbow," said Delores. "*He* should talk!"

"Well, I've got a solution," said Bernie. "We could introduce the guy in 107 to Felicity Jones. Then maybe they'd marry and move out."

"And maybe they wouldn't. Maybe they'd stay right here and raise a lot of little nut cakes, and *then* where would we be?" Delores picked up the tweezers and attacked her eyebrows once again.

Bernie sighed and leaned back against the desk. Out of the corner of his eye, he thought he caught something flutter behind the drapes to the dining room. But though he walked around the whole lobby, checking the drapes and the lampshades and behind each sofa and chair, he could not find the bat that had come in Felicity's window and which, he was sure, was still there.

A SLIGHT DISTURBANCE

It wasn't too early to start thinking about costumes for Halloween, Bernie decided. Stores in Middleburg had changed their window displays from school notebooks and lunch boxes to cobwebs and skeletons. Even Mrs. Magruder was thinking how to decorate the lobby of the Bessledorf Hotel for Halloween.

"What are you going to be this year, Bernie?" Georgene asked him on the way to school. Bernie, Georgene, and Weasel usually thought up their costumes together. One year Georgene dressed up like Dorothy in *The Wizard of Oz,* while Bernie was the Scarecrow and Weasel, the Tin Man.

Another year Georgene's mother made her a costume that looked like a hamburger on a bun. Bernie came as a French fry and Weasel was a bottle of ketchup. But costumes like those were hard to make, and even more difficult to wear when the kids went out trick-or-treating. This year they wanted something simple.

"I think I'll be a bandit," said Georgene. "Just a mask over my eyes or something."

"I've got an old sailor hat of my uncle's," said Weasel. "That's enough costume for me. Or maybe I'll just wear a white shirt and a tie. Now *that's* scary!"

Joseph had said he could get a white lab coat for Bernie to wear over his jacket, so Bernie said he'd go as a veterinarian.

Lester, however, insisted on going as a milk shake, and Mrs. Magruder said he could tie a pillow over his head for the whipped cream, a red ball on top of that for the cherry, and a piece of plastic pipe sticking out of the top of his jacket for the straw.

"You know," Mrs. Magruder told her children, "there was a letter to the newspaper from the Society for the Protection of Homeless Cats, warning people to keep their pets in till Halloween is over. It said that some people steal cats and dye them black to use at Halloween parties, and you know how Lewis and Clark would take to that! I let those cats out two nights ago and haven't seen them since. I think you ought to go looking for them, Bernie."

"Cats do have a way of wandering off and coming back home again," said Joseph.

"If they wandered off to somebody else's house, would that be so bad?" said Delores. "I think I could do very well without stepping over their litter box in the bathroom, brushing cat hair off my skirt, listening to them yowl outside at night, and having them leap on my lap when I'm sitting on the couch with a boyfriend."

With the thought of Indiana Aztec bats flying around Middleburg, however, Bernie didn't like the idea of the cats being outside at night, so he did what he always did when the cats were missing: took Mixed Blessing, who slept on the doormat inside the lobby, and went out to look for them. Lester tagged along.

They went up and down alleys in Middleburg, calling their names: "Lewis!" Bernie would call.

"Clark!" Lester would cry.

And, as usually happened, they didn't have to go far. When they reached the alley behind the library, Mixed Blessing walked a little faster and then began to trot. He nosed about behind a pile of trash and found Lewis and, hiding behind a garbage can, Clark. The cats seemed rather happy to be discovered, in fact, and snuggled up against the boys' jackets when Bernie and Lester picked them up.

"What would happen if one of our cats got bitten by a bat, Bernie?" asked Lester. "Just a common ordinary bat, I mean."

"They'd have to test the bat for rabies," said Bernie.

"How would they do that?"

"Cut off its head, I think."

Lester was quiet for a moment. "What if Clark was bitten by a bat and you couldn't find the bat? How would you know if Clark had rabies? Would you have to cut off *his* head?"

"Let's don't talk about it," said Bernie.

As they walked back home toward the hotel, however, the brothers could tell that something strange had happened, for people were pouring out the front door, some in their night clothes, and several of the women were holding newspapers over their heads and screaming.

Bernie looked up, expecting to see flames leaping from the roof. But the hotel appeared perfectly fine to him. As he pushed his way inside, he could see no fire, smell no smoke.

Theodore Magruder was standing on a chair trying to calm everyone down, but he could not be heard above the noise. Salt Water, the parrot, was flapping from perch to table to sofa to perch again, squawking, "Duck and cover! Duck and cover!" and Delores cowered in a corner with an umbrella over her head.

"What's happening?" Bernie asked when he reached his mother.

"The bat!" she answered. "It fluttered right across the lobby, Bernie, and people are panicking. They are absolutely hysterical!"

At that moment Joseph came down the hall holding his butterfly net high in the air, and in the net was a small brown bat, helplessly flapping its wings.

"Ladies and gentlemen!" cried Mr. Magruder, much

relieved. "The bat has been captured! You have nothing to fear but fear itself, I assure you!"

A few people, upon seeing the bat, turned to listen. Others stopped pushing their way toward the exit and reconsidered. Delores, in fact, abandoned her place in the corner and came over to ring the bell on the registration desk and get the attention of the crowd.

"Ladies and gentlemen!" Theodore tried again. "You are now residing in the finest hotel in the state of Indiana, and it is our aim, our hope, indeed, our *pleasure*, to keep you safe within our walls. Even as we speak, ladies and gentlemen, even as we *speak*, our son Joseph, the renowned student of veterinary medicine, eventually to be the renowned *Doctor* Joseph Magruder, has captured the bat that simply made a slight detour in its flight plan and entered our hotel through an open window."

People parted to let Joseph and the butterfly net through the throng, the bat ensnared in the mesh.

"Even as we speak," Theodore went on, "the bat will be placed in a secure container and transported straight away to the veterinary college where it will be studied by learned professors from all over the world. So there is nothing to fear, ladies and gentlemen, nothing at all. Please return to your rooms and dine on your dinners, bubble in your baths, browse your books, plump your pillows, dunk your doughnuts. . . ."

"Dad," said Bernie, pulling at his sleeve.

". . . and enjoy your stay at the Bessledorf," finished his father.

The people in the lobby began talking among themselves, debating whether they should check out of the hotel or stay, but slowly, one by one, then two by two and three by three, they began moving back down the corridors to their rooms, and those on the sidewalk came back inside.

They were all invited to free coffee in the dining room, where they stood about talking and laughing a little at their own foolishness. Finally the lobby was empty once again except for the regulars—Mrs. Buzzwell, Mr. Lamkin, and Felicity Jones.

Joseph came up from the basement holding a large mason jar with holes punched in the lid. Inside was the small brown bat, very ordinary looking, like a mouse without a tail, its little beady eyes looking at Bernie through the glass.

"Is this the ferocious Indiana Aztec?" Bernie asked his brother.

"As far as I can tell, it's a common garden-variety bat that will do you no harm," said Joseph. "I'll find out for sure when my professors have a chance to inspect it tomorrow."

"Well, if it's not an Indiana Aztec, what is it doing here now?" asked Mr. Lamkin.

"Bats are looking for places to hibernate this winter;

that's why we're seeing them. It's perfectly natural; perfectly normal. The bats are simply doing what bats are supposed to do," Joseph told him.

"I don't know what kind of bat it is, Mr. Magruder, but I think this hotel should be bat-proof," said Mrs. Buzzwell, her three chins wobbling as she spoke. "No one likes to go to bed at night with the thought that she might wake up the next morning with a bat in her hair."

"Or worse, not wake up at all," said Mr. Lamkin.

"With a vampire bat clinging to your throat by its teeth," said Felicity Jones in a small, shaky voice.

"That business of a bat getting in your hair is all a myth, Mrs. Buzzwell," Theodore told her.

"Now, I don't know about that," said old Mr. Lamkin, looking at Mr. Magruder over the tops of his glasses. "Back in 1926 . . . or was it 1927? . . . a bat got in my great-aunt Minnie's hair, and the only way they could get it out was to shave her head."

"Oh, Mr. Magruder," said Felicity Jones, "I fear I am the cause of this disturbance. If only I had left my window closed when I composed my ode to the moon, the bat wouldn't have flown inside, and this never would have happened."

"Well, it's water over the dam," Mr. Magruder told her. "Compose all you want, my dear, but keep the window closed."

"And your mouth shut," Delores murmured under her breath, but only Bernie heard.

Eventually even the regulars sauntered off to their rooms, leaving only the Magruders in the lobby. And then the phone rang. Theodore answered, but the voice on the other end was so loud that Bernie knew right away who it was: Mr. Fairchild, from Indianapolis, owner of the Bessledorf Hotel.

"Theodore, what's this I just heard on the news?" he asked. "Guests were fleeing a thirty-room hotel down in Middleburg because of a rare species of bat called the Indiana Aztec? Is this what I'm going to see on TV tomorrow—a picture of our guests standing outside my hotel in their pajamas?"

"It's all taken care of, sir," said Mr. Magruder.

"And how is that, Theodore? You've given them robes?" bellowed the owner.

"No, sir," said Bernie's father. "The bat has been caught, and Joseph will take it to the veterinary college for an examination."

"I don't care if the bat has been given an honorary degree! What about our *guests*, Theodore? Our *guests*?"

"They are all in bed, sir, sleeping like little lambs."

"Lambs about to be slaughtered, I would imagine. What do you know about this Indiana Aztec bat?"

"Not much, sir. Only what the posters tell us." And here Mr. Magruder told his boss what was on the posters all over town. "But we will be extra cautious not to leave any windows or doors open until this blows over," he said.

"Well, see that you don't. The last thing Middleburg needs is a quarantine because of some brainless bat who ended up here instead of South America. If they can't migrate to the right continent, for heaven's sake, what good is sonar?"

"I believe they were on their way up here, sir. Once every seventy-five years, we understand, the bats leave their nests in South America and migrate to Indiana."

"Now who put *that* idea in their heads!" said Mr. Fairchild. "Whatever, let's keep our guests as innocent as babes in the woods, Theodore, and see if we can't keep this whole thing hush-hush. Good night."

"Very good, sir. Good night," said Theodore. And even as he spoke, a bat outside flew past the window, silhouetted against the moon.

FRONT PAGE

With the election only four weeks away, terrible arguments were going on in Middleburg. Bernie's sixth-grade class was studying history and government, and every day the teacher talked about the coming election for mayor.

The people who were voting to keep the present mayor, Clementine Carlson, wanted more trees in the park, more books in the library, and they loved the church bells playing "Abide with Me," every hour on the hour.

The people who were going to vote for Harold Higgins wanted fewer laws, lower taxes, and they wanted to get rid of "Abide with Me," the bells along with them.

When there were town meetings to hear the candidates talk, Clementine Carlson's supporters would sit on one side of the auditorium and shout, "More trees! More trees!" and Harold Higgins's supporters would sit on the other side chanting, "Lower taxes! Lower taxes!" And soon the auditorium would be filled with shouts of

"Bells, yes!" or "Bells, no!" Sometimes it got so raucous that Officer Feeney was called in to keep order.

"I don't know," he said, walking alongside Bernie as they circled the block. "Those ding-dong bells are causing more trouble in this town than Eleanor Scuttlefoot ever imagined, I'll wager. Once people's sleep is disturbed, why, all sorts of things could happen."

"How about old Mr. Scuttlefoot himself?" Bernie asked. "What does *he* think about all the trouble those bells have caused?"

Officer Feeney ran his nightstick along the wooden pickets of a fence. "That's the funny part. Back when the Scuttlefoots first married, those bells only played on Sunday mornin's. But now that Eleanor's dead, those doggone bells have to play 'Abide with Me' every hour on the hour for as long as her husband lives, and by this time, he's deaf as a doornail and don't even hear all that dingin' and dongin'. It's the rest of the town, not him, that's rememberin' Eleanor Scuttlefoot, and not thinkin' very kindly of her either."

Feeney was right about that, because the very next day there was a protest march around city hall, demanding that the bells come down.

Three times the protestors marched around city hall shouting, "Down with the bells!" and holding signs that read, ABIDE SOMEWHERE ELSE.

🦇 🦇 🦇

When a picture of the marchers was published on the front page of the newspaper the next day, Theodore Magruder was shocked to see his very own daughter at the front of the line waving a sign that read:

Ding dong dong,
No more song!

"Delores, my girl, have you lost your senses?" he fumed at the supper table. "The Bessledorf is here to serve *everyone,* the dingers and the no-dingers alike. The dongers and the anti-dongers! We simply cannot take sides in public, and you, being the oldest of my children, should know that already!"

"*I'm* not the manager of this hotel!" Delores argued. "*I* have a right to be heard."

"The acorn doesn't fall very far from the tree, my girl, and people will assume that if you are against the bells, you got your views from me!" Theodore said.

"What's he saying, Bernie? That he's a nut?" Lester asked.

"What I'm saying," Theodore declared, "is that if Mr. Fairchild sees this picture, I may be fired from my job as hotel manager, and this family will once again be . . ."

". . . blowing about the country like dry leaves in the wind," said Mrs. Magruder, weeping. "Delores, how *could* you?"

But before Delores could answer, the phone rang. Bernie knew right away it was Mr. Fairchild.

"Let's don't answer," said Lester. "I don't want to be a dry leaf in the wind."

"We could say we were all at church listening to the beautiful bells," said his mother.

"You don't have to go to church to hear those confounded bells!" Delores declared as the phone jangled again. "They can probably be heard all the way to Indianapolis."

Mr. Magruder, of course, picked up the phone and immediately Mr. Fairchild's voice filled the room.

"Theodore, what the ding-dong-dong is your daughter doing on the front page of the newspaper?" he bellowed. "The Bessledorf Hotel never takes sides! The Bessledorf is to remain as pure and impartial as the driven snow! The Bessledorf . . ."

"Oh, stuff it!" Delores muttered over her meat loaf.

"I heard that!" came Mr. Fairchild's voice.

"I'm sorry, sir," said Theodore. "But I fear that my daughter has temporarily taken leave of her senses. I have scolded and lectured and preached and protested, Mr. Fairchild, but if you ever had a twenty-year-old daughter, perhaps you can sympathize with me."

"I don't have a daughter, so I can't sympathize, Theodore, but now that she's done what she did, you'll have to balance it out. There's to be another protest march on Saturday, I've heard, to *keep* the bells, and I want one of your other children to march in *that*."

"It will be done, Mr. Fairchild. My word is as good as my bond, and I shall leave no stone unturned," Mr. Magruder told him.

"Whatever," said Mr. Fairchild. "But it isn't enough for your kid just to march in that parade; make sure he gets his picture in the paper too!" And Mr. Fairchild hung up.

Joseph backed away from the table. "Don't look at me, Dad. Saturdays are our busiest days at the veterinary college. It can't be me."

Theodore looked across the table at Lester, who had mustard on his upper lip, gravy on both cheeks, and ketchup on his chin. "No," Theodore said, and turned to Bernie. "It's up to you, my lad, to save the family. I want you to march in that protest parade on Saturday carrying a sign that says you love the bells."

"But I don't! I hate the bells!" said Bernie. "That's a lie, Dad. Do you want me to *lie?*"

"Oh, Theodore, you can't ask our child to be untruthful!" cried Mrs. Magruder. "We are doomed! *Doomed,* I tell you!"

Bernie looked about him uncertainly. He didn't like to see his mother cry or his father worry, but he especially didn't like the thought that his father might lose his job and they would have to leave Middleburg and his friends. Yet how could he carry a sign he didn't believe in? Not only that, but he had to get his picture in the newspaper.

"I'll think of something," he told his father.

"That's the spirit, Bernie!" said Theodore. "I knew I could count on you. The acorn doesn't fall very far from the tree, all right, and big oaks from little acorns grow."

Bernie wished he would leave off with that nut stuff. He had enough problems on his hands without worrying about acorns, too. Suddenly he wasn't hungry anymore. He went out to the registration desk and called first Georgene, then Weasel.

"I've got big problems," he said, and told them what his father wanted him to do.

"We'll think of something," said Georgene. And they did.

When Saturday came and the "Save Our Bells" group gathered in front of the church to march down Bessledorf Street, there was Clementine Carlson at the front of the march, followed by a man and woman holding a CLEMENTINE FOR MAYOR sign, followed by people waving SAVE OUR BELLS flags, and at the very end walked Bernie Magruder. He was holding a leash, and at the end of the leash was Mixed Blessing.

There was a sort of blanket draped over the Great Dane's back, like a horse blanket. On either side, in big

45

black letters, were the words, I GO NUTS OVER BELLS.

And that was the truth, because every time the bells started playing "Abide with Me," Mixed Blessing did go a little nuts, barking and howling and whining and pacing. But sure enough, the photographer who showed up to take a picture of the march took a picture of Clementine Carlson at the front of the line, and Bernie, with Mixed Blessing, at the back.

"Excellent, Theodore!" Mr. Fairchild said when the picture appeared in the Indianapolis paper the next morning. "I want you to frame both pictures and hang them in the lobby of the hotel until this election is over. This will show our customers that we are fair and square—that both sides are represented in my hotel, and no matter how a person may care to vote, he will find a home and kindred spirits at the Bessledorf."

In all the controversy over the bells, the bats had almost been forgotten, but they weren't very far from Mrs. Magruder's mind.

"Joseph, what did they say at the veterinary college about the bat you captured here?" she asked as they passed the scalloped potatoes at dinner.

"The professors called in the most renowned authority on bats in the state of Indiana, and he says that bat is an ordinary brown bat, common to the midwestern states, and it isn't unusual for them to be coming

46

indoors, looking for places to sleep over the winter, so we've nothing to worry about," Joseph said.

"A common ordinary bat! I'm so relieved!" breathed his mother.

"*Unless,*" Joseph continued, "there is still an invasion of bats coming our way from South America. And though it's unlikely that there is a species that the professors don't know about, it's still possible that the Indiana Aztec does exist, which is why the professor asked me to collect any other bats that might find their way into our hotel and bring them in for observation."

"Well, how long will it take them to get here, for heaven's sake?" asked Delores. "How long do I have to wear a football helmet when I go outside?"

"My dear, dear family," said Theodore. "Let us not get our britches twisted in an uproar. Let us not let our wits get the best of us and go off with our brains half scrambled. Let us—"

"Look!" cried Bernie suddenly, his eyes on the window. The family turned, their eyes in the direction Bernie was pointing.

There was the belfry of the Bessledorf church silhouetted against the purple of the night sky. And darting here and there, backward and forward, up and down, in and out, were a half dozen bats, circling the belfry, and coming back inside again, probably to roost.

Seven

A New Development

The Magruders weren't the only ones staring out a window. When they went into the lobby, the regulars—old Mr. Lamkin, Felicity Jones, and Mrs. Buzzwell—were gathered at another window, watching, too.

"Mr. Magruder, do you see what *we* see?" rasped Mrs. Buzzwell.

"They're just bats, Mrs. Buzzwell, and nothing to get excited about," Theodore told her.

"Bats are simply looking for somewhere to sleep this winter, and a church belfry is as good a place as any," Joseph explained.

"But I don't ever remember bats in our town before," said Felicity.

"That's because you weren't paying attention. Try not to let it distress you, my dear. Come summer, the more bats we have, the fewer mosquitoes there will be to bother us," said Theodore, "for bats are great insect eaters."

"They are just simple, ordinary brown bats," said Mrs. Magruder. "Joseph said so."

But Joseph, Bernie noticed, stood at the window after the regulars had gone back to their places at the card table, his eyes on the belfry, his lips pressed together in thought.

Meanwhile, the arguments for and against the bells were growing stronger. When people came to church, in fact, the pro-bell people sat on one side of the church and the no-bell folks sat on the other. When people came to the Bessledorf Hotel for dinner, Mrs. Magruder had to ask them where they wished to be seated—the pro-bell section or the no-bell section.

Clementine Carlson went on TV and promised that if she were reelected, the bells in the Bessledorf belfry would stay, and Harold Higgins promised that if he were elected, the bells would come down.

BAN THE BELLS signs went up next. Harold Higgins himself and his campaign manager rode through the streets with the windows rolled down, and Higgins spoke to bystanders through a bullhorn: "I pledge to you," he called, "that if I am elected mayor, my first order of business will be to dismantle those bells."

"People are listening to him, Theodore," Mother said that evening when the family gathered for dinner. "Perhaps we ought to vote for him for mayor. We have to do something to save our town."

"Don't be too hasty, Alma," said her husband. "I've just come from a town council meeting and, according to the lawyer for Eleanor Scuttlefoot's estate, if those bells stop playing 'Abide with Me' while her husband is still alive, not only will he and any children they might have forfeit their inheritance—which would be considerable—but the town must give back the bells in the belfry, the new church carpet and stained glass windows that Eleanor Scuttlefoot paid for, as well as five new desks in the library, three new slides on the playground, the fountain in the park, the brick sidewalk along the river . . ."

". . . and a partridge in a pear tree!" said Delores. "Big deal! Eleanor's husband is deaf as a post and couldn't hear a bell if one fell on his head. What good is a desk and a slide and a fountain and a sidewalk if half the town has gone mad and people aren't speaking to one another?"

"Patience, my girl," said her father. "We must not rush blindly into decisions and revisions, which a moment could reverse. We must not let our premonitions determine what our course of action will be. Now is the time for all good men to come to the aid of their party, and . . ."

"Oh, Theodore, for once in your life talk sense!" his wife cried suddenly as "Abide with Me" rang out over the air. "Those bells are beginning to get to me, too. If you were at the town council, why didn't you speak up and say that something must be done?"

"Don't you remember what Mr. Fairchild said, my dear? That we are not to take sides?"

"I don't care a fig what Fairchild says!" cried Mrs. Magruder. "My head aches, my teeth hurt, my jaws are sore, and my nerves are shot from listening to those ghastly things!"

Bernie got up from the table and went into the lobby to take Mixed Blessing out. He did not like to hear his parents quarrel, and whenever it seemed they were about to have an argument, he cleared out as fast as he could.

Quarreling made the cats nervous too. There were times Bernie felt sure that Lewis and Clark could understand everything that was being said and just pretended they were mere cats, ignorant of human conversation. Now they paced nervously around the lobby, and even Salt Water seemed agitated.

"Quiet, please! Quiet, please!" the parrot squawked.

Bernie went outside and walked the Great Dane as far as the library, then crossed the street to the drugstore and started back toward the hotel again. There was a clean crisp feel to the night air—the smell of burning leaves and fireplace smoke, of dead wood and fresh apples. It was then he saw Officer Feeney standing in the shadows of an old house in the middle of the block. He could tell right away that the policeman did not want anyone to see him.

Bernie went up the brick sidewalk to the house and right smack over to where the policeman was standing.

"Hi, Officer Feeney! What are you doing back here in the shadows?" he asked.

"Shhhh," said the policeman, reaching out and pulling Bernie behind the bushes with him. "Don't you know better than to say hello to somebody who's stakin' out the territory?"

"What territory?" asked Bernie.

"I'm not about to go givin' away trade secrets to anyone, least of all you," the policeman said.

But Bernie knew that Officer Feeney liked nothing better than talking about his work to anyone who would listen, and he knew just how to worm it out of the policeman. So he said, "Oh, I get it. You were demoted, weren't you? And you've been assigned to keep cats out of flower beds or something."

Officer Feeney bristled. "I should say not! It's not like that at all! You know whose house this is, don't you?"

Bernie looked up. "It's old Mr. Scuttlefoot's, isn't it?"

"Righto."

"So are cats digging in *his* flower bed, or what?"

"Worse than that, my boy! Much worse than that."

"*Dogs* are digging in his flower bed?" asked Bernie.

The policeman leaned down. "What would you say, Bernie, if I told you that I have been assigned to keep my eye on this house because of . . ." He leaned even closer until his mouth was right beside Bernie's ear: "because of *death* threats."

"Death threats!" cried Bernie. "Against old Mr. Scuttlefoot? Why would anyone want to hurt him?"

"Why indeed?" said the policeman. "Because guess what happens if somebody shoots him through the heart?"

"He dies?" said Bernie.

"Right," said Feeney. "And what happens if old Mr. Scuttlefoot dies?"

"He gets buried?" said Bernie.

"More than that."

"He goes to heaven?"

"*Think*, Bernie, *think!*" said the policeman. "Never mind Mr. Scuttlefoot. What happens in town?"

Bernie's eyes grew wide. "The bells can stop."

"Right. Once Mr. Scuttlefoot is gone, Eleanor had no reason to keep 'Abide with Me' playing every hour on the hour so he wouldn't forget her, and Middleburg's long ordeal is over. So somebody just decided to hurry things along, I guess, because a note was slipped under the old man's door this mornin' that read: *If the bells don't stop, you do!* And it's up to me, Bernie, to protect the gentleman and find out who's tryin' to do him in."

"Only half the town, Feeney," said Bernie. "Only half the town."

He took the dog back to the hotel and, waiting for

53

Mixed Blessing to lift his leg one more time beside the azalea bush, glanced up at the sky to see if the bats were circling the belfry again.

And there they were, just as before, except this time something was different. Something was very, very different. Bernie stared intently, trying to figure out what, and then he saw it: A pale green light rose from the church belfry and disappeared like fog into the night air.

Bernie tumbled into the lobby with Mixed Blessing, let go of the dog's collar, rushed past Delores who was sitting at the registration desk with a movie magazine propped up on a large bowl of popcorn, and ran back to the Magruder apartment, where his parents were still having a heated discussion.

"Look!" he cried, grabbing them both by the arms. "Hurry! Go to the window and look."

His parents stopped talking immediately, and Joseph and Lester came over to see also, as Delores wandered in from the lobby. The entire family crowded around the window and stared at the church belfry, which towered above the funeral parlor next door.

It was unmistakable now: A pale light rose from the belfry, like a cloud of vapor, and it was a ghastly, ghostly green.

Eight

DOWN FROM THE SKY

Once again, the Magruders weren't the only ones staring out the window, for the regulars could smell trouble a mile away. Within minutes old Mr. Lamkin, Mrs. Buzzwell, and Felicity Jones were crowding around a window in the lobby, and they, too, stared at the green glow in the sky. Felicity, in fact, tilted slightly to the left as though she might faint.

"Mr. Magruder!" Mr. Lamkin shouted. "Those are not common ordinary brown bats! The Indiana Aztecs have arrived, and they're roosting in the church belfry!"

"We'll have to abandon the town!" Mrs. Buzzwell shrieked in a voice that sounded like gravel going down a tin chute. "The president will have to send in the National Guard."

Felicity Jones simply tilted a little *too* far to the left this time and fell in a faint on the floor.

"Oh, Theodore!" cried his wife. "It's just as the warnings said: You can tell an Indiana Aztec by the pale green light rising from its roosting place. They've come, and they've chosen the belfry. And if anyone disturbs their habitat, he'll die!"

"I think they ought to give the whole town a month's vacation, and spray the place from one end to the other," said Delores, fanning Felicity until the thin young woman opened her eyes once again.

Once Mrs. Buzzwell knew about the pale green glow in the church belfry, the whole town knew it. Now the authorities were frightened, but no one wanted to come right out and say that the Indiana Aztecs had settled in Middleburg, because it was sure to be bad for business. Travelers arriving at the bus depot wouldn't know whether to stay or leave. There was even a rumor that the body currently residing in the drive-through window of the Bessledorf Funeral Parlor was there because it had been bitten by an Indiana Aztec.

Bernie and his friends stood on a street corner and looked up at the night sky.

"Maybe it always looks this way in October," Georgene said hopefully. "Maybe it doesn't have anything at all to do with bats."

"Maybe it's the aurora borealis," said Weasel.

"Yeah, and maybe it's your grandfather's mustache," said Bernie. "We all know those bats are Indiana Aztecs, so why doesn't somebody do something about them?"

"Are you kidding?" said Georgene. "Who's going to crawl up there and try?"

At school the next day, Bernie, Georgene, and Weasel stood on the playground talking with the other children. All anyone wanted to talk about were the bats in the church belfry.

"My dad says that if they're in the belfry now, they'll be in our attics next," said one girl.

"Mine says that if Clementine Carlson is reelected, the bells will probably drive us all crazy, so the bats won't matter," said another.

Suddenly Weasel cried, "Look!" and all faces turned toward the sky. And then the playground was filled with screams and cries, everyone running every which way, for coming down out of the sky, right into the playground, in fact, was the largest bat Bernie had ever seen. Its wingspan was at least eight feet, its body as black as midnight, with a small head and round ears.

Everyone else seemed to be screaming and running for cover. The principal, in fact, came to the door of the school and blew a whistle for everyone to come inside. But something held Bernie's feet to the spot as the monster bat came closer, even though there were sirens in the distance and police cars racing toward the school.

And then Bernie saw a parachute open above the giant wings, and the colossal bat did not dip and dart as bats do, but came gliding right down onto the concrete. As the costumed man got to his feet, Bernie saw that on the parachute was printed in big black letters, ACE EXTERMINATORS, WHEN YOU WANT THE BEST.

Officer Feeney came rushing into the school yard as the parachutist was trying to untangle his lines, and two police cars came screeching to a stop.

"Sorry!" called the man in the bat costume. "I was supposed to land in the field out there, but the wind carried me onto the playground."

"Let me see your permit," said the chief of police as he got out of his car. "A cheap trick, if you ask me, using the townfolks' fear of the Indiana Aztec to advertise your company."

"Talk to the owner, not me. I'm only doing my job," the parachutist said.

The principal was blowing her whistle hard now and motioning for Bernie to come in, so he walked over to where Georgene and Weasel were standing, and they all went in together.

"For a while I thought we were goners," said Weasel. "The bat looked like it was going to crash right into us."

"This town is going nuts, Bernie. Absolutely nuts," Georgene said.

Bernie liked having something special to tell his family when he got home from school. Usually the older ones in the family had all the news, and he and Lester just listened. Delores would have tales of what had gone on at the parachute factory, Joseph would have a story of something that had happened at the veterinary college, and Dad or Mom would have a funny joke to tell about one of the guests. This time *he* would have a story.

But when he turned the corner of Bessledorf Street with Georgene and Weasel, they saw an ambulance in front of the hotel.

"Old Mr. Lamkin must have seen that parachutist and had a heart attack!" Bernie said, hurrying toward the entrance. He didn't want to consider the possibility that it might have been his mother or father, because he didn't know what he would do if anything happened to them.

"Here comes somebody," Georgene said, for the glass doors of the lobby swung open just as they reached the hotel, and out came the attendants carrying a stretcher, and on the stretcher lay Felicity Jones, her arms folded over her chest.

Mrs. Magruder followed the men outside and stood wringing her hands at the open door of the ambulance while they lifted the stretcher and put Felicity inside.

"Please take good care of her," Mrs. Magruder told the men. "I don't want to have to call her parents and give them bad news about their daughter."

"We'll do our best, ma'am. She's got a pulse, which

means her heart is beating, and where there's a heart, there's hope," one of the men said.

Bernie, Georgene, and Weasel rushed up to Mrs. Magruder.

"What happened?" Bernie asked.

"It's Felicity," said his mother. "I was just sitting at the registration desk working on my new novel, when Felicity Jones, as white as a sheet, walked into the lobby and announced that she had been bitten on the neck by an Indiana Aztec. And then . . . she just collapsed on the floor in front of me!"

The hotel was in an uproar. No matter how Mr. and Mrs. Magruder tried to keep it quiet, the news spread quickly, and soon there were reporters and photographers snapping pictures of the Bessledorf Hotel, popping into the lobby to ask who was Felicity's closest of kin, what her symptoms were, and what she had eaten for breakfast.

"Please!" begged Theodore. "When we know anything for certain, I will be sure to let you know. Meanwhile, let us not run off at the mouth and start rivers of rumors while we are still wet behind the ears."

"Huh?" said a reporter.

"What did he say?" asked another.

"He said 'Wait and see,'" Bernie interpreted.

When Joseph came home from the veterinary college, he had to push to make his way inside the hotel, and when Delores returned from a hard day at the parachute factory, she took her football helmet and hit a few reporters over the head with it in order to get to the door.

"What the heck is going on?" she called to Bernie. "Has this whole town gone crazy?"

"Miss? Miss?" called a reporter. "Are you friends with the woman who was bitten by an Indiana Aztec in the hotel?"

"Buzz off," said Delores. "Go chase a fire engine or something."

Bernie held the door open till she got inside, then closed it again in the reporters' faces.

"What idiotic thing has Felicity done now?" asked Delores. "It *was* Felicity, wasn't it?"

"She claims she was bitten by a bat, and they've taken her to the hospital," said Mrs. Magruder. "What a trying day this has been!"

Bernie had just opened his mouth to tell them about the parachutist when Lester crowed, "Yeah, some guy in a bat costume parachuted into the school yard today, and—"

"Lester, *I* wanted to tell about that!" yelped Bernie.

"And he used one of *our* parachutes too!" said Delores. "If we had known what he was going to do with it, we never would have given our permission."

So much for his story, Bernie thought. The only way *he* would ever have something exciting to tell was if *he* were bitten by an Indiana Aztec, only then he probably wouldn't be around to tell it.

Nine

A WEIRD DISCOVERY

Just after dinner, when Bernie had gone out into the lobby again, the glass doors suddenly opened and in came Theodore Magruder, escorting Felicity Jones on his arm. He led her over to a chair and sat her down.

Like a pack of wolves, the reporters and photographers swarmed in after them and began snapping one picture after another: Felicity opening her eyes, Felicity closing her eyes, Felicity yawning. . . .

"Good grief," said Delores. "So she's alive! Big deal! Why don't you take a picture of somebody *interesting* for a change?" And she sat up straight in her chair and crossed her legs, balancing one shoe on the end of her toe.

"Will she *live?*" called out a reporter, holding a notebook and pencil.

"Could the bite have been fatal?" called another.

"Is it contagious?" still another wanted to know.

"My good people, please do not tie yourselves in knots. Our dear Felicity Jones just comes from a somewhat sensitive family, and as the twig is bent, so grows the tree."

"Huh?" said the reporters.

"It seems that in the current warm spell, a lingering mosquito from our hot wet summer had somehow managed to survive, and as our dear guest Felicity Jones lay in repose upon her bed in serene slumber, the inhospitable mosquito did awake and proceed to nip her on the neck."

The photographers crowded in so close to get a picture of the small red welt on Felicity's neck that she recoiled in horror.

"It was only a mosquito bite, my good people," Theodore assured them. "A minute mosquito bite of the smallest proportions, nothing less, nothing more."

And suddenly old Mr. Lamkin stood up at one end of the hotel lobby and cried, "And now if you will get the ding dong out of this lobby, perhaps we can get some peace and quiet, and I can finish watching my favorite show, *No Tomorrow*."

Disappointed that there wasn't a bigger story than this to report, the reporters and photographers filed out again and drove away.

"Oh, how I wish all this were over!" Mrs. Magruder said, and turning to her oldest son, she asked, "Joseph, have you found out *any* more at all on the Indiana Aztec at the veterinary college?"

"Nothing," said Joseph. "My professor has written to the leading authority on bats in South America to see if there is a species we don't know about, but so far we haven't had a reply."

"There was an emergency meeting of the town council today," said Theodore, "in which we called in three exterminating companies to consider the possibility of getting rid of the bats in the belfry, just in case, but not one of them would touch it. Not even the Ace Exterminating Company. They say they would be glad to tackle a single bat in someone's attic, maybe, but they won't go near the church belfry with its pale green glow. They would not risk one of their employees receiving a fatal bite by disturbing the habitat of the Indiana Aztec."

"Well, this is a fine state of affairs!" said Delores. "Half the town is going crazy because of the bells in the belfry, and nobody can disconnect them without crawling up there, which no one will do because of the bats."

"Somebody has to actually crawl up in the belfry to deprogram the bells?" asked Joseph.

"That's what I heard at the parachute factory," said Delores. "Eleanor Scuttlefoot sure did a number on us. She made sure that the controls for the bells were up in the belfry so that no one could easily slip in the church at night and shut the danged things off."

🦇 🦇 🦇

Later, Bernie found Joseph standing at the window once again, staring out at the church belfry and the bats that flew around it. Lewis and Clark had hopped up on the windowsill, and they, too, were watching the bats, their jaws quivering with just the thought of holding one of those darting creatures in their mouths.

"What's your best guess, Joseph?" Bernie asked. "Do you think those are Indiana Aztecs or not?"

"I don't know what to think," said Joseph. "Nobody seems to know who put those notices up around Middleburg, but what I'm seeing here is certainly different from any other bat I've ever known. The way they fly, for one thing. I can't explain it exactly, but the way they dip and dive . . . it's too jerky to be any of the bats around here."

"Somebody ought to crawl up there in a space suit and capture one of them," said Bernie.

"Don't you get any ideas," Joseph told him. "A space suit might save you from one solitary bat, but not if the whole swarm attacked you."

Okay, he wouldn't even consider crawling up there, Bernie thought as he zipped up his jacket and went out into the evening air, where the bells were just ending the nine o'clock playing of "Abide with Me." But what about if he brought home a little bat dung for Joseph to analyze? Surely some bat, at some point, might have dropped a little on the ground below, and that might tell a great deal about the species if it could be examined under a microscope.

He had asked Georgene and Weasel to meet him at the church, but he didn't say why. He was afraid they might not come if he told them, and he was almost right.

"You want us to help you look for bat poop?" Weasel said. "Bernie, it's dark out here, it's forty degrees, and I could be home watching TV and drinking hot chocolate."

"Fine," said Bernie. "Good night, Weasel." He knew his friend wouldn't leave him, not as long as Georgene was staying.

"For your information," Georgene told him, "it's not called poop. If it's from a bat, it's called *guano,* and it's very valuable stuff because it's sold for fertilizer."

"So why didn't you say so?" said Weasel. "We'll come out every night looking for guano and make a million bucks." He pushed his glasses back up on his nose and stared hard at the ground.

They had each brought flashlights, too, as Bernie had instructed, and they spread out around the church, searching every square inch of earth. But the ground was dark and wet and covered with leaves, and Bernie soon realized that even if he found some, he wouldn't know it because he had no idea what *guano* looked like.

He began to feel very foolish. He always seemed to be asking his friends to help with projects that usually turned out to be weird. They had been good sports to help him change the sheets in all the hotel guest rooms looking for bats, and here they were, once again, looking for poop.

Bernie was just about to tell them that the search was off, that Weasel could go home and enjoy his hot chocolate, when suddenly Georgene said, "Hey, what's this?"

Bernie and Weasel came over. Georgene was holding something in her hand that was thin and black and about six inches long. It appeared to be the wing of a bat.

Georgene gasped. "Oh, m'gosh!" She said, and handed the bat wing to Bernie.

"What kind of bats are these if they fall apart?" Weasel asked, his eyes huge, directing the beam from his flashlight on the thing in Bernie's hands.

"Plastic, that's what!" said Bernie. "It's *plastic*!"

Indeed it was. The black plastic wing of a toy bat.

"But it looks so real!" said Georgene. "You don't suppose . . ." She looked up toward the sky where the other bats were circling.

"It could all be coincidence—somebody out here playing with a toy bat for Halloween," said Weasel.

"But we don't think so!" said Bernie, speaking for all three of them. "Somebody's up there with remote-control bats. *That's* why Joseph thought they were flying funny."

"And if that's true, then the green light is probably fake too," said Georgene.

"Let's go tell Officer Feeney!" said Weasel excitedly. "We'll bust this story wide open! We'll get our pictures on the front page of the newspaper!"

"No!" said Bernie, thrusting the wing in his jacket pocket. "Not until we find out who it is. I don't want to just hand this story over to Feeney and let him get the credit. If we find out who's behind this, we'll have solved the whole thing, and we'll *really* be famous. We'll go down in the *Guinness Book of World Records* as the youngest detectives ever to solve a case, I'll bet."

"And if we decide to be detectives when we're grown," added Weasel, "and they ask what mysteries we've solved, we can say, 'You remember the case of the Indiana Aztec bat, don't you, back in Middleburg, Indiana? Well, that was us. That was a case we solved.'"

"So who *would* be behind this?" asked Georgene. "It doesn't make much sense. Obviously, as long as the town thinks there's a dangerous colony of bats up there, nobody's going to crawl up to deprogram those bells. But the person who most wants to keep those bells ringing is Eleanor Scuttlefoot herself, and she's dead."

Just then the bells played the first four notes of "Abide with Me," marking the quarter hour. Bernie and his friends stared up at the belfry looming above them. Who *would* want to keep those bells ringing?

"Her ghost?" said Weasel.

Ten

BATS IN THE BELFRY

Bernie had a lot of thinking to do. A *lot*. If the wing they had found was off a plastic bat, and if the bat was operated by remote control, and if the remote control was up in the church belfry—then it meant, in short, that somebody was trying to frighten the town for whatever reason Bernie didn't know, trying to make the people of Middleburg believe that dangerous bats had come up from South America to settle here. The big question was, should he tell Officer Feeney about it? It troubled him all the way to school the next day.

Bernie wanted so badly to solve this mystery himself—with a little help from his friends, of course. He told himself that if the wing were simply off a kid's plastic toy and had nothing to do with the bats circling in the sky above, then he would have wasted Officer Feeney's time for nothing, and weren't policemen busy people?

I'll wait until I'm sure that somebody's up there in the belfry, and then *I'll tell Feeney about it,* he decided as he stared at the blackboard, scarcely hearing what the teacher was saying.

If those bats *were* operated by remote control, somebody was pretty good at it. Somebody not only had a fantastic remote device and a light that cast a green glow, but a key to the belfry as well.

Second thought: *Maybe you didn't need a key.* The minister never locked the church. The doors were unlocked all the time so that people could come in and pray. For all Bernie knew, somebody might be camped up there day and night in the belfry, playing with a remote control.

"Bernie?" said the teacher.

Bernie blinked his eyes. "South America?" he said quickly.

Everyone laughed, and Bernie's face reddened.

"We're through with geography, Bernie. We're on history now," the teacher said. "The question was, 'What city was the first capital of the United States?'"

"Oh," said Bernie quickly. "Uh . . . New York?"

"I think somebody needs to do some catching up," said the teacher. "I'm going to send a note home to your parents, Bernie, asking that you put in at least another hour on homework each night."

Bernie groaned under his breath and had to forget about bats for the time being.

🦇 🦇 🦇

"Boy, did *you* get in trouble!" Georgene said as they walked home that afternoon, kicking at the leaves on the sidewalk. There were even leaves stuck in her ponytail.

"I know," said Bernie.

"He's got bats in the belfry, that's what," Weasel joked.

"If I'm right about those bats being operated by remote control, it's got to be somebody who's pretty good with that kind of stuff," Bernie said. "Somebody who's got a whole remote-control setup."

"Who do we know who can operate six bats all at the same time?" asked Weasel. "One or two racing cars, maybe, or even a couple of airplanes, but not a whole swarm of bats at once."

"There's only one way to find out," said Bernie. "We've got to go up in the belfry and see."

Georgene stopped and stared at Bernie in horror. "No, Bernie! What if we're wrong? What if they really are Indiana Aztecs, and we disturb them?"

"All we'll do is go up the stairs to the belfry," said Bernie. "Just stand outside the door and listen. We won't open it or go out there or anything."

Weasel tried to act brave. "And if the bats ask you what we're doing up there, we'll say we're sorry for intruding, but they forgot to put a DO NOT DISTURB sign on their habitat."

"W-when are we going to do it?" Georgene asked.

"It had better be this weekend when no one's around, because *next* weekend is Halloween, and everyone will be out on the streets. Someone would be sure to see us going inside the church," Bernie said.

"This weekend, meaning . . . ?"

"Tonight," said Bernie. "Tonight, before we chicken out."

"Before *you* chicken out, Bernie. I'm not going up there," Georgene told him. "I'll stay down below, though, and be your lookout if you want."

"Yeah, Bernie," said Weasel. "There's probably not room in that belfry for two people. I'll go as far as the stairs with you."

"That's okay. If it gets too hot to handle, we'll let Officer Feeney in on it," Bernie told them.

"What time do you want us to meet?" asked Georgene.

"I usually walk the dog around nine," said Bernie. "Let's meet then. One of you can stand outside with Mixed Blessing."

"Oh, Bernie, I'm scared," Georgene confessed. "What if you're attacked by the bats? What if one of them bites you? What if you become the first victim in Middleburg, and Weasel and I just stood there and let it happen?"

"Just tell people I wanted to save the town and there was no way you could stop me," Bernie said bravely. "I'll see you tonight at nine." And they separated at the corner, each going home to his own house—Bernie to the Magruders' apartment there at the Bessledorf.

At nine that night, Bernie said, "I think I'll walk Mixed Blessing now, Mom."

"I just walked him, Bernie," said Joseph. "He's in for the night."

"Oh," said Bernie. His pulse began to race. What excuse did he have now to go outside in the dark?

"Are Lewis and Clark in for the night, Mom?" he asked.

"I don't want them out at all until Halloween's over, but I think Mr. Lamkin let them out when he went to the park this afternoon," his mother said. "Check on them, will you?"

Bernie gave a quick look around the apartment, then the lobby, and though Lewis was sleeping peacefully in an armchair, Clark was not in sight. He could, of course, be in a number of different places, including the basement, but Bernie didn't bother to look.

"I can't find Clark, Mom," he called. "I'm going out and look around the neighborhood, okay?"

Mrs. Magruder was writing the second chapter of *Lusty Eyelids* and didn't even look up. "Don't be long," she said.

Bernie put on his jacket and baseball cap and went outdoors.

"Clark!" he called, though not very loudly, and was glad that the cat didn't immediately appear. He thrust his hands in his jacket pockets and hurried up the street toward the church.

Georgene and Weasel were already there, huddled inside the doorway, shoulders hunched against the wind.

"Why didn't you go in?" Bernie asked. "Are the doors locked?"

"I didn't even try them," said Georgene. "I didn't think we should walk right in."

"Yeah," said Weasel. "We figured we'd let you go in first in case anybody's in there and wants to know what we're doing. Where's the dog?"

"Joseph already walked him. I'm supposed to be looking for Clark." He looked around. "Clark!" he called softly. He opened the big door of the church a crack. "Clark!" he whispered. "Well, he didn't come. I guess we'll have to go inside and check."

Pulling on the big brass handle of the mahogany door, Bernie swung it open all the way. There was a dim light in the ceiling of the foyer, and another, high overhead, above the altar at the far end of the aisle.

"Where are the stairs to the belfry?" Georgene whispered.

"Behind the choir loft," Bernie whispered back, as though they might be bothering someone if they spoke out loud.

Bernie went first, followed by Georgene, then Weasel—past the altar, around the choir loft, to the little brown door. When he opened it, it gave a slow *creeeaaak*. Inside was a narrow, curving staircase, as dark as a cave.

"Darn!" Bernie whispered. "I forgot my flashlight. All I can do is feel my way ahead of me."

Weasel, who had said he would stay at the bottom of the stairs, and Georgene, who had claimed she would wait outside, could not help themselves: With Bernie in the lead, they followed him into the dark passage.

"W-what do you feel?" Georgene whispered over Bernie's shoulder.

"Mostly cobwebs along the wall," he said.

"But won't the belfry door be locked when we reach the top?" Weasel asked.

"I don't know," Bernie answered. "It's supposed to be. If it's locked, that means nobody's up there. Not right now, anyway. But if it's unlocked . . ."

"Then we're dead meat," said Weasel.

Bernie's knee and forehead hit the wall at the same time where the stairs were curving.

"Steer right," he whispered back over his shoulder. The boards creaked beneath them as they made the turn. Keeping their hands out on either side to feel the walls, Bernie and his friends continued up—step over step, step over step—up and up and around and around.

And then Bernie saw it—a pale green glow coming

from beneath a door at the very top of the staircase. He stopped in his tracks, making Georgene bump into him from behind, and Weasel bump into her.

"L-Look!" said Bernie.

"Do you hear anything?" Weasel whispered. "Does it sound like bats?"

"I don't know," Bernie answered. "What do bats sound like?" He slowly went on up the stairs to the top and put his ear against the door. "All I hear is a sort of buzz. . . ."

Suddenly, before he could catch his breath, the door above him swung open and in the brightness of the light, bats came dipping and darting toward him.

Now Weasel was first in line as Bernie and his friends went skidding and sliding back down the narrow stairs, righting themselves halfway down, and leaping and stumbling the rest of the way until they fell in a heap by the choir loft.

For a moment Bernie lay with his arms around his face to protect him from bat bites. When nothing happened, he peeked out at Georgene and Weasel and together they sat up and looked warily around.

"Man!" gasped Weasel. "They were all *over* the place, Bernie!"

"Did anybody get bitten?" asked Georgene.

"I don't think so," said Bernie. "But we disturbed their habitat, all right."

"Well, we disturbed something, anyway," said Georgene. "But we still don't know if they were real or not."

"Maybe the whirring's just the sound of their wings," said Weasel.

"I think someone heard us coming and opened the door to scare us," said Bernie. "Maybe we should go back up there and see who it was."

"Are you *crazy*?" Georgene and Weasel cried together.

"If there really are bats there, next time they'll attack!" said Georgene.

"They'll follow you home, Bernie. They'll see where you live and invade the hotel!" warned Weasel. "They'll be waiting for you in your closet and under your pillow. They'll even hide in the toes of your socks."

Whatever the truth, Bernie decided, it was enough of a scare for one night. So they slipped out of the church and closed the door behind them, hardly saying a word all the way to the corner. Bernie's heart was still thumping so hard in his chest that it hurt, and his pulse was racing.

"I . . . I don't think I've ever been so scared in my whole life," Georgene said finally.

"Me either," said Weasel. "We came *that* close to being bitten. I'm not going back up there for anything in the world. I'm not even going near those stairs."

"I'm not either," said Georgene. "I want to see my picture in the paper, but not in a coffin!"

The truth of the matter was that Bernie was too frightened to go back to the belfry himself. But he *did* want to know what was up there. He *did* want to solve the mystery himself for a change, without Officer Feeney butting in and taking the credit.

They whispered a while longer when they reached the corner, and then Bernie said good night to his friends and walked home alone, his eyes on the sky. Clark was sitting on a chair just inside the door when Bernie came in. Bernie leaned over to pet him, and Clark purred, but his eyes seemed to say, *You were up to something, Bernie Magruder. Don't get me involved in all this!*

Eleven

FLUTE SCOOTT

"What's the matter with you, Bernie?" his sister asked the next day at the breakfast table as she buttered a biscuit, covered it with raspberry jelly, then delicately licked the red stuff off her finger. "You haven't said one word. You haven't even fought with Lester over the comics."

"I'm thinking," said Bernie, staring down into his shredded wheat.

"Well! That's a change!" said Delores, and dipped her spoon once more into the jelly jar.

"My dear!" said Mr. Magruder. "Do not underestimate a thought! A journey of a thousand miles begins with a single step."

"So?" said Delores. "What's that got to do with anything?"

"And do you know what it takes to make that step?"

"A foot?" said Lester from his end of the table.

"A thought!" said his father. "A thought directs the foot that takes the step that makes the journey that . . ."

". . . lives in the house that Jack built," finished Delores.

Joseph, however, studied Bernie from across the table and slowly raised one eyebrow, as if to question him. But Bernie, not wanting to tell anyone, not even Joseph, what he knew about the bats in the belfry, thrust his spoon in his cereal and took a bite.

"Theodore," said his wife. "We simply must start decorating the lobby for Halloween. All the other businesses on Bessledorf Street have their jack-o'-lanterns out already, and Mr. Fairchild will want to know what we have done to make the hotel festive."

"How about a gallon-size dish of candy corn on the registration desk?" said Lester, licking his lips.

"We could put costumes on the animals," suggested Joseph.

"How about a witch outside?" said Bernie. "The kind that looks like she flew right into a telephone pole?"

"I think we should spray cobwebs all over the lobby," said Delores. "Especially over those chairs in the corner where the regulars play cards. I swear, Mother, sometimes it looks as though Mrs. Buzzwell, Felicity Jones, and old Mr. Lamkin don't move from day to day. They're playing cards when I get up in the morning, and they're still there when I go to bed at night. The only break they take is when Mr. Lamkin stops to watch *No Tomorrow* on the TV."

"Well, I can think of a lot worse things they could be doing," said Mr. Magruder. "Be charitable for once, Delores."

"I *am* charitable," said Delores. "I just want to be sure they're alive."

"I will need a dozen pumpkins," Mrs. Magruder went on, addressing her husband. "And if Mrs. Verona doesn't want to carve them into jack-o'-lanterns, we could have a carving contest in the hotel dining room some afternoon."

"I shall order whatever we need," said her husband. "Pumpkins, cornstalks, witches, whatever. You be in charge of decorating, my dear, and I shall see that there are plenty of treats for the little ghosts and goblins who will be paying us a visit."

Breakfast over, the family set to work on their Saturday chores, for every Magruder had to help out on weekends.

Lester's job was to empty all the wastebaskets and separate aluminum cans from the rest. Bernie was supposed to carry all the clean sheets and towels from the laundry to the linen room.

As he walked down the hall, his arms stacked with towels, Bernie passed room 107 and saw that the DO NOT DISTURB sign was still on the door. Thoughtfully, he stacked the towels on the top shelf of the linen room, the sheets on the next, washcloths on the third shelf, with pillowcases below. What if the man in 107 *did* become a regular and never let anyone in his room? He could be making bombs in there, and no one would know until the hotel blew up.

When he had finished his work, Bernie went back out to the registration desk where Delores was trying to polish her toenails, one bare foot propped on the rim of the wastebasket.

"I want to see the registration book," he told her.

"Help yourself," his sister said, waving her little brush toward the book on the counter. "Just don't bump my arm, please."

Bernie opened the book to the day's date, and then began leafing backward through the pages, looking for the day that someone signed into room 107. Who was this guy, anyway?

There were some pretty weird names in the guest book, he realized, but that's always the way it is in a hotel. Along with ordinary names such as Nancy Brown or John Smith, there was a Mary Christmas, a Georgia Peach, a Jack Spratt, and Pete Moss. But there, beside Room 107, was the strangest name of all: Flute Scoott.

Wait a minute! Bernie thought, checking the day the man had signed in. Wasn't that about the time the posters appeared all over town, warning about the bats? Bernie counted backward on his fingers till he figured out the day he and Officer Feeney had seen the first one. Flute Scoott had registered at the Bessledorf Hotel the day before. Bernie's heart began to pound.

He went around the desk and into the apartment, where he called Georgene and Weasel.

"Meet me in the lobby," he said, and was waiting for them when they rode up on their bikes.

They sat in a row on the leather couch near Salt Water's cage, and Bernie told them what he was thinking. "The warning signs about the Indiana Aztec bats began going up around town the day after Flute Scoott registered at our hotel," he told the others.

"Lots of people registered at your hotel that day," said Georgene.

"And he won't let Hildegarde in to clean his room," Bernie continued.

"So what does that prove?" asked Weasel.

"And he goes out for a walk every night at the same time, Delores said, and comes back a few hours later."

"Bernie, half your guests go out to dinner every night. They don't all eat at the hotel," said Georgene. "I think you're really stretching it!"

"I don't care, we're going to sit right here and wait for him. We'll follow him tonight when he goes out, and *I'll* bet he'll head for the church around seven o'clock."

"Bernie, you're crazy! That's nine hours away!" Weasel cried. "I can't sit here for nine hours! I'd grow roots!"

"What we should really do is wait till he leaves, and then check out his room," said Georgene.

"We can't. That's one thing I can never do: go in a guest's room without permission," Bernie said.

Wilbur Wilkins, the hotel handyman, came in with a wheelbarrow full of pumpkins, a heap of cornstalks on top, and Mrs. Magruder scurried around pointing out just where each should go—a pumpkin here, a cornstalk or two there. Delores followed with a spray can of artificial cobwebs—*poof, poof*—until there were cobwebs hanging from lamps, light fixtures, doorways, picture frames, and before anyone could stop her, there were cobwebs covering old Mr. Lamkin, Mrs. Buzzwell, and Felicity Jones as well. When Mr. Lamkin, astounded, opened his mouth in protest, the cobwebs stretched and looked like a mosquito net over his mouth.

There were cobwebs on Salt Water's cage, cobwebs on Lewis and Clark's tails, and cobwebs between the ears of Mixed Blessing, who was sound asleep on the rug. The big dog startled and yawned and sat up, looking surprised to see how the hotel lobby had been transformed.

Suddenly, however, the dog rose up stiffly, his ears erect, nose twitching. He looked toward the hallway. Bernie and Georgene and Weasel looked, too, and there was the young man from room 107.

He did not seem especially pleased to find Delores at

the registration desk again—with little balls of cotton between her toes—and Delores was not particularly pleased to see him.

"Yes?" she said, blowing on the wet polish on her toenails.

The man from room 107 was holding a wastebasket filled to overflowing with soft-drink cans, sandwich wrappers, and empty cookie and potato chip containers.

"I want to empty my wastebasket," the man said. "If you'll just tell me where to dump it."

"All you have to do, Mister, is leave it in your room and Hildegarde will empty it for you when she changes the sheets," said Delores.

"I don't want anyone in my room," the man said. "Just tell me where I will find the Dumpster, and I'll empty it myself."

"Be my guest," Delores said, and pointed him toward the side door.

Bernie nudged Georgene and Weasel, and when Flute Scoott had gone back to his room, the three rose from the couch, went outdoors, and climbed up the side of the Dumpster.

Bernie lost his grip and slid back down again, and Georgene wasn't tall enough to see over the top.

"What do you see, Weasel?" she called, still clinging to the side.

Weasel had worked his way up to the top and had his

arms clamped over the edge. "An empty bottle of mouthwash, a couple razor blades, a cracker box," said Weasel. And then he yelled, "Eureka!"

"What? What?" asked Bernie.

"A worn-out lightbulb," Weasel said. "And it's painted green."

Twelve

THE SHADOW

"We still don't have a case, Bernie," Georgene told him. "It's not against the law to hang a DO NOT DISTURB sign on your door. It's not illegal to own a green lightbulb or take an evening walk."

"There's enough evidence to make a person suspicious, though," said Bernie.

"But what's the motive?" Georgene went on. "Even a man suspected of murder has to have a motive."

"Let's think," said Weasel, climbing up on the wall behind the garden, letting his legs dangle down the other side. "If this guy really is behind the warnings about the Indiana Aztec, and he's really flying remote-control bats from the belfry, then *why*?"

"Duh!" said Bernie. "That's what we're trying to figure *out*, Weasel!"

Bernie and Georgene climbed up on the wall, too, and sat on either side of Weasel.

"Maybe he's not flying them from the belfry. Maybe he's flying them from his room, and that's why he doesn't want anyone in there," Weasel suggested.

"His room's on the other side of the hotel from the belfry," said Bernie.

"Oh, right," said Weasel. "Scratch that." He thought some more. "Okay, let's make some guesses. Why would Flute Scoott want to scare everyone with remote-control bats?"

"To drive us nuts," said Bernie. "Maybe he wants to make a ghost town out of Middleburg. If word got out that the Indiana Aztec bat had formed a colony in our belfry, nobody would want to move here, and everyone in Middleburg would leave."

"But why would he want that to happen?" asked Georgene. "Why would he want a ghost town?"

"Because it's Halloween?" Weasel joked, but nobody laughed.

"So what are we going to do, Bernie?" Georgene said. "If we're not going to turn that green lightbulb over to Officer Feeney, and you're going to try to solve this mystery without him, don't you go around telling people you solved it all by yourself. We're helping too."

"Naturally," said Bernie, holding out his hand. "Just give me the lightbulb, Weasel."

But Weasel wouldn't let go. "Nope," he said. "Just so you remember we're in on this too, I'm keeping at least some of the evidence myself."

🦇 🦇 🦇

The rest of the day was ordinary. All the Magruders worked at decorating the lobby, so that by evening, the place was aglow with grinning jack-o'-lanterns, scowling jack-o'-lanterns, sad, happy, suspicious, and playful orange faces that leered at the hotel guests from every corner, every table, every shelf, and windowsill. They were lined up along the registration desk, perched on top of the TV, and sat in clusters on the floor.

Salt Water scolded the pumpkin faces, Lewis and Clark hissed as they went by, and once, when Bernie heard Joseph yell, *"No!"* he saw Mixed Blessing start to lift one leg over them.

Bernie was waiting for the man in 107 to come out of his room and take his evening walk, when, at that very moment, the glass doors to the lobby swung open and in came old Mr. Scuttlefoot, looking very perturbed indeed. He was wearing a long gray coat with a gray hat on his head. He had a cane in one hand, and he almost stumbled over the Great Dane who came over to sniff him.

Bernie, who had just strung an artificial cobweb from a lamp to a light switch, turned to stare as the old man ducked behind a fern, then darted behind a pillar, and finally hid himself behind the drapes in the doorway to the dining room.

Bernie looked at Joseph, Joseph looked at Delores, and Delores twirled her finger around beside her ear to show that Mr. Scuttlefoot had a screw loose some-where. But Mr. Magruder rose to the occasion. He got up from behind the registration desk, adjusted the carnation in his lapel, and casually strode over to the doorway.

"Ah, good evening, Mr. Scuttlefoot!" he said to the drapes, which were looking rather lumpy. "And a very good evening it is!"

Nothing moved.

Theodore stepped even closer to the drapery, and this time he spoke even louder. "GOOD EVENING, MR. SCUTTLEFOOT. HOW MAY I BE OF SERVICE?"

This time the drapery wiggled, and finally a nose emerged, then a chin, and eventually the little man stepped out where the family could see him.

"Eh?" he said.

"HOW MAY I HELP YOU?" Theodore shouted.

"You may help me by calling the police," said Mr. Scuttlefoot. "I believe my life is in danger, for I am being followed."

"IS THAT SO?" said Mr. Magruder, trying not to frighten the animals with his shouting. Lewis and Clark were already twitching their tails.

Mr. Scuttlefoot tapped his cane on the floor. "Yes, it is, and I want protection. Everywhere I go, there's a shadow here, a shadow there; shadows, shadows every-where! Somebody wants me dead."

Mrs. Magruder came over and gently touched his arm. "My dear Mr. Scuttlefoot, now who would want to harm a nice old man like you?"

"What?" said Mr. Scuttlefoot.

Mrs. Magruder put her mouth to his ear. "WHO WOULD WANT TO HURT YOU?" she asked.

"I don't know," the old man said, nervously twirling his cane, "but it's because of the bells. My neighbors don't seem to like me much anymore."

"Imagine that!" said Delores.

"Oh, Mr. Scuttlefoot, the town is only doing what your deceased wife requested, but it's certainly not your fault," Mrs. Magruder told him.

"Of course not!" said Delores, who was trying to calm down the cats, who were pacing now. "It's not his fault that the bells clang and clunk every fifteen minutes. It's not his fault we have to listen to them night and day until we all go deaf or bonkers, whichever comes first."

"Eh?" said Mr. Scuttlefoot, cupping his ear. "Did she say 'bombers'? Are they trying to bomb me now?"

"No, no, no!" said Mrs. Magruder. "Please sit down, Mr. Scuttlefoot, and we will bring you a nice cup of tea."

"Eh?" said the old man. "They're coming by sea?"

At that moment the glass doors of the lobby swung open once more, and in came Officer Feeney.

"There he is!" the policeman said, spotting Mr.

Scuttlefoot. "I've got the assignment to keep my eye on Mr. S. here, and I'll be danged if he don't give me the slip. Why, he's like a slippery eel, he is—dartin' in doorways, hidin' under stairs, slippin' behind trees, goin' down alleys. . . ."

"Officer! Officer!" cried Mr. Scuttlefoot. "I want that man arrested!"

"What man?" asked Feeney, looking around and seeing only Bernie and Joseph and Lester.

"Eh?" said Mr. Scuttlefoot.

"WHAT MAN?" yelled Officer Feeney.

And Salt Water shrieked, "Cut the racket! Cut the racket! Awk! Awk!"

"The man who has been following me," Mr. Scuttlefoot yelled back.

"It's *me* who's been followin' you, Mr. Scuttlefoot," said Officer Feeney. "Though I'll admit, there may be one or two people in Middleburg who'd like to take a shot at you to stop those blasted bells."

"What's that?" Mr. Scuttlefoot said. "Somebody wants to shoot me?"

"Surprise, surprise!" said Delores dryly. "I'll be a raving lunatic if I have to listen to those bells much longer."

Bong! Bong! Bong! came the bells, followed by the first few notes of "Abide with Me." Delores covered her ears, then threw back her head and howled at the ceiling, and Mixed Blessing immediately joined in.

At that moment Felicity Jones came down the hall holding a lighted candle and reciting a poem by Edgar Allan Poe:

> "... keeping time, time, time,
> In a sort of Runic rhyme,
> To the tintinnabulation that so musically wells
> From the bells, bells, bells, bells,
> Bells, bells, bells,
> From the jingling and the tinkling of ..."

"Is this a madhouse?" asked old Mr. Scuttlefoot, looking from Delores to Felicity to the howling dog and now the cats and parrot.

"Sometimes I wonder that myself," said Officer Feeney to the old man. "Come along, Mr. Scuttlefoot, and let me escort you home."

When the two had gone, Mrs. Magruder gave a sigh of relief. "Perhaps *now* we can get on with Halloween," she said.

Bernie looked around. "Has that guy in 107 gone out for his walk yet?" he asked his sister.

"With all this going on tonight, you think I paid attention?" Delores said.

Just then Bernie discovered that Mr. Scuttlefoot had left his cane behind, hooked over the back of a chair. He picked it up and hurried out the front door to see if he could catch up with him and Officer Feeney. He could see them far down the block, heading for the big house where the Scuttlefoot family had lived for five generations with their dozen or more cats.

But as he trotted along, he noticed a shadow on the other side of the street, a man who seemed to be matching his steps with those of Mr. Scuttlefoot and Officer Feeney. If they stopped, he stopped. When they went forward again, so did he.

It could, of course, simply be someone out for an evening walk. It could be a member of the Society for the Protection of Homeless Cats, looking for homeless cats to protect. But somehow Bernie didn't think so, for the man ducked into doorways and stepped behind trees, and finally turned a corner and disappeared for good.

And suddenly Bernie had another thought. A terrible thought. Maybe the man in 107 hadn't come to town about the bats at all. Maybe he was here about the bells. And maybe, just maybe, someone had hired him to do away with Mr. Scuttlefoot.

Thirteen

PLAYING THE GAME

Halloween fell on Saturday this year, and at school the day before, all the classes held their annual Halloween parties, Bernie's sixth-grade class included. Everyone came to school in costume, and just as they'd planned, Georgene came as a bandit with a black mask over her eyes; Weasel came as a sailor in his uncle's navy hat; and Bernie wore a white lab coat he had borrowed from Joseph, to dress as a veterinarian.

Of course, no one did much work because ghosts kept peeking in each other's classrooms, skeletons rattled down the halls, witches rode their broomsticks around the playground, and zombies walked stiff legged through the lunch room.

By afternoon, everyone gave themselves over to having fun. There were games and refreshments, and in Bernie's room, they voted on the scariest costume, the most original, the funniest, the best homemade.

There were doughnuts and cider and little paper cups filled with black and orange candy. Finally, because there were still twenty-five minutes left before school was out, the teacher wrote the word *Halloween* on the blackboard. The game was to see how many smaller words each student could make by scrambling the nine letters in Halloween.

Bernie didn't especially care for pencil games. He much preferred being out on the playground. Weasel, however, chewed on his pencil for a moment, then wrote down a few words, and chewed some more.

It was Georgene who liked word games. Bernie watched her pick up her pencil, and she never stopped writing till the teacher called, "Time!" And it was Georgene, of course, who found more words than anyone else:

HALLOWEEN		
hall	eel	won
all	now	wean
law	how	lean
lawn	heel	allow
low	no	ale
awe	on	owe
wall	halo	lane
new	hello	lone
whole	well	one
hole	wheel	alone
when	howl	noel

"How did you get so many?" asked Bernie. "I only got eleven."

"I got fourteen," said Weasel.

"I got thirty-three," said Georgene, who was the winner indeed, and she said she could have got even more if she'd had time.

When school was out, the kids gathered on the playground to chase each other around in costume or try on one another's masks and just generally whoop it up. It didn't seem fair that now that they were dressed, they had to wait another whole night to go trick-or-treating. But when the bells began to chime four o'clock, everyone scattered and tried to make it home before they had to listen to "Abide with Me" ring out over the city.

Mrs. Magruder was wearing her usual black hostess dress with pearls, ready to seat guests as they came down to dinner. She was teaching the parrot to say, "Welcome! Come in!" when suddenly the glass doors of the lobby swung open and in came Mr. Scuttlefoot again, looking even more agitated than he had the night before.

"Now what?" said Delores, rolling her eyes.

Mixed Blessing saw the old man stumbling through the doors just in time, and got out of the way. Mr. Scuttlefoot moved toward the door of the dining room, grabbed Mrs. Magruder by both arms, and begged her to let him eat in the hotel that evening.

"It's a matter of life or death," he croaked, "for I fear I am being poisoned."

"Oh, Mr. Scuttlefoot, who would want to poison a kind old man like you?" Mrs. Magruder asked.

"Eh?" he said, cupping one hand over his ear. "They've put it in my stew?"

"NO, NO, NO!" cried Mrs. Magruder. "I SAID, WHO WOULD POISON A KIND OLD MAN LIKE YOU?"

"The cook, maybe?" he answered. "Or maybe the fella at the grocery store. But I've got pain in my feet, pain in my jaw, pain in my shoulder. . . . It's *poison*, I tell you!"

"Well, of course you can eat here tonight," Bernie's mother said as Bernie led the man to a table far back in one corner. And she added, "I'll bring you a nice bowl of tomato aspic."

"Arsenic?" Mr. Scuttlefoot cried in horror as the guests at another table turned and stared.

"NO, NO, NO! ASPIC! TOMATO ASPIC!" said Mrs. Magruder. "Please, Mr. Scuttlefoot, sit down and be quiet. You're scaring our customers with your wild imagination."

Officer Feeney came in just then, and Mrs. Magruder quickly led him over to Mr. Scuttlefoot's table.

"You've got to sit down with him and keep him quiet," she whispered. "I'm afraid it's not just his hearing that's going, but his mind as well."

Officer Feeney shook his head. "I hate to say it, Mrs. Magruder, but there are folks here in town who would be just as happy if the old man *did* kick the bucket, if that's the only way to stop those dang-donged bells."

"Well, that's your problem, Officer Feeney," said Bernie's mother. "Right now *my* problem is to keep the Bessledorf dining room a quiet and pleasant place to have dinner."

"I'll do my best," the officer said. "But do bring me a piece of that lovely veal with a dish of white beans on the side, if you please."

There certainly were a lot of mysteries here to solve, Bernie was thinking as he went back out in the lobby. Like was there really such a thing as the Indiana Aztec bat? And who was up there in the belfry, and who was trailing old Mr. Scuttlefoot, and was someone really poisoning his food?

If, by tomorrow night when Halloween was over, he decided, he still wasn't any closer to solving the mystery, then he would tell Feeney what he suspected—Feeney or Joseph or his father or *some*body. Except he wasn't too sure *what* he suspected. Maybe he *couldn't* solve the whole thing by himself, but at least he wanted to be able to tell them enough so that he and Georgene and Weasel could get their names in the paper as playing a part in the investigation. Perhaps they'd get their pictures on the front page as well!

He lay on the top bunk in the bedroom he shared with Lester. His brother was eating potato chips in the bunk below, and Bernie knew he wouldn't sleep until all the crunching and lip smacking was through. He thought about all the things that had happened since his family had moved in to manage the hotel. If his mother wanted to write a book, why didn't she write about some of those—the ghost and the pirates and the face in the Bessledorf Funeral Parlor? Why did she have to write books with titles like *Quivering Lips* and *Trembling Toes*? Stupid titles like *The Passionate Pocketbook* and *Lusty Eyelids*?

"Bernie," came Lester's voice from below. "Do you think it's true that a person can go crazy just listening to those bells?"

"I don't know," said Bernie. "I guess our town is about to find out."

"When you go nuts, do you know it?"

"I suppose you think everyone else is crazy but you."

"Then how do we know we're not crazy already?" asked Lester. "How do we know we're not all acting just a little bit strange and nobody realizes it?"

"We don't. For all we know, Middleburg is just one big zoo," said Bernie, "and scientists are wandering around town in disguise, studying us."

There was quiet for a while in the bedroom. Then Bernie could hear Lester's breathing become deeper and more regular. Finally a sleepy voice said, "Bernie, if I ever go completely nuts and forget my favorite pizza, it's pepperoni and sausage with onions, okay?"

"Okay," said Bernie.

"And don't forget to feed my frog . . . ," Lester said, his voice trailing off.

"What frog?" asked Bernie. When Lester didn't answer, he had to ask it again. "What frog, Lester?"

"In . . . my . . . bottom . . . drawer . . . ," Lester murmured.

"Good grief," said Bernie.

Lester fell asleep, but Bernie had too many things on his mind. Too many unanswered questions. He thought maybe he was about to drift off when he heard something scratching against the windowpane. Could it be a bat, trying to get in? Lester's frog?

Bernie opened his eyes and stared up into the dark, listening some more. Now the scratching had become a soft *tap, tap, tap.*

Bernie threw off the covers and climbed down from his bunk. He made his way over to the window without turning on any lights.

"Georgene!" he whispered in surprise when he saw her standing there in the moonlight in her bathrobe and pajamas.

They whispered through the open window.

"I wanted to call you, but I was afraid I'd wake your

folks," Georgene told him. "Guess what?"

"What?"

"It's about Flute Scoott."

"What about him?"

"Scramble the letters, Bernie."

"*What?*"

"Scramble the letters and see what you get."

"Georgene, it's dark in here. It's after eleven o'clock. Just tell me!"

"Okay. I don't know why I didn't think of this before, but if you mix the letters of both names together and rearrange them, Flute Scoott is just another name for Scuttlefoot."

Fourteen

BATMAN

Bernie, Georgene, and Weasel huddled in one corner of the hotel dining room after all the guests had had breakfast, and tried to decide what to do.

The newspaper that morning said that the town council had passed a resolution that the bats in the church belfry were to be left undisturbed; that the town would not risk the lives of any of their workers to remove them. Both candidates for mayor, Clementine Carlson and Harold Higgins, agreed on that. And now that Bernie and his friends knew that the letters in Flute Scoott also spelled Scuttlefoot, they wondered what it all meant.

"What do you think is going on?" Bernie wanted to know. "Is the guy who's crawling up in the church belfry, playing with remote-control bats, really old Mr. Scuttlefoot in disguise?"

"That's stupid," said Weasel. "I'd guess it's the other way around. It's old Mr. Scuttlefoot who's in disguise. Maybe he's not old at all. Maybe the real Mr. Scuttlefoot died a long time ago, was buried in the family's backyard, and nobody knew it. Maybe the man we *think* is Mr. Scuttlefoot is an impostor, an actor. Maybe the *real* Mr. Scuttlefoot died before his wife, and she buried him in secret, just because she wants the bells to go on playing her favorite hymn forever, which the town agreed to do as long as her husband lived."

That was something Bernie hadn't thought of yet. "Well, if old Mr. Scuttlefoot was buried in his backyard, we should be able to find his grave," he said. "There's always a lump or a hump or a mound or a marker of some kind."

"I think you're both full of baloney," put in Georgene, reaching for another doughnut that Mrs. Verona, the cook, had placed on the table along with steaming mugs of hot chocolate. Bernie's hotel was the best place to meet in the whole wide world, his friends thought.

"Do you have a better explanation?" Bernie asked.

Georgene didn't, but she still thought it was a dumb idea. "If old Mr. Scuttlefoot is a fraud—if he's really an actor going around in disguise, living in the Scuttlefoot house and playing old man by day and staying here and playing with mechanical bats at night—then he's hood-winked us all," she said.

"But in case Weasel *is* right—that the real Mr. Scuttlefoot is buried in their backyard—let's snoop around there tonight while we're out trick-or-treating," said Bernie. "And whatever we find, or if we don't find anything more—we'll tell Officer Feeney once Halloween is over."

"Why do we have to wait till it's over?" asked Weasel.

"Because if we tell what we know now—what we suspect, anyway—that the bats in the belfry are operated by remote control, probably someone hired by the Scuttlefoot family, the store owners will be angry at all the business this has cost the town. They'll want to organize a posse, they'll probably cancel the parade, and no one will be giving out treats in all the confusion. If we get anything at all, it will be pennies and carrots and little boxes of raisins," Bernie explained.

That was certainly true.

"Okay," Georgene agreed. "But tomorrow we all—Weasel and I, too—go see Officer Feeney and get our pictures in the paper."

"Of course," said Bernie.

So for the rest of the afternoon, anyway, they gave their attention to Halloween and added a bit more to their costumes. To her half mask, Georgene added a striped sweater; to his sailor hat, Weasel added a pipe in the corner of his mouth and pasted a tattoo on his arm, like Popeye; Bernie added a stethoscope around his neck to look like a real veterinarian.

Lester dressed himself up as a piece of Swiss cheese, his body sandwiched between two sheets of yellow cardboard filled with holes.

Everyone in the Magruder family, of course, dressed for Halloween to greet the guests and the tourists and all the trick-or-treaters who would visit the hotel that evening. Theodore himself dressed up as Abraham Lincoln, with a black stovepipe hat, a false beard, and a black coat.

Mrs. Magruder was Little Bo Peep in a full skirt and bonnet, carrying a staff in her hand.

Joseph was Dracula, complete with long fingernails and fangs.

And Delores, of course, dressed in a tall witch's hat, a black dress, and black fingernails and lipstick.

Then there was Mrs. Verona, who had put on a tall white chef's hat; Wilbur Wilkins, the handyman, dressed as a scarecrow; and Hildegarde, the red-haired cleaning lady, who had always wanted to be a ballerina. She went from room to room with her broom and bucket, wearing a pink tutu and pink slippers. Bernie noticed that when she stopped outside each room and called out "Housekeeping," she then whirled around three times before making her grand entrance.

The Magruders and the rest of the hotel employees went to the second floor to watch the Halloween parade from the front windows. All the town officials were in it, waving to the crowd, followed by floats from the Lions Club, Kiwanis Club, and Veterans of Foreign Wars. A long line of police cars came next, then fire trucks, and finally the Middleburg High School marching band.

There was a pumpkin princess who threw candy corn to the crowd, and assorted dancers and trumpeters and ghosts and witches. Mixed Blessing barked at all the confusion, Salt Water squawked, and the cats hid behind the sofa and wouldn't even come out to watch.

As afternoon became evening, Mr. Magruder went about lighting all the jack-o'-lanterns, Mrs. Magruder set out trays of licorice sticks, Mrs. Verona brought in a fresh batch of chocolate cookies to give away as treats, and then the Magruders retired to the kitchen for a light supper before the trick-or-treating began.

Bernie was just finishing the last of his hamburger when suddenly a shadow appeared at the back door window, blocking the light from the porch, and the family saw the doorknob begin to turn. Suddenly the door flew open and a masked man appeared in the doorway.

Delores screamed, Lester dived under the table, and just as Mr. Magruder rose to protect his family, in came Mr. Fairchild, the owner, dressed as Batman—the mask, the cape, the boots—everything.

"Happy Halloween!" he said. "I see we are all in the spirit of the holiday! Marvelous decorations, Theodore! Simply magnificent, Alma! I hope that every room has been booked for the festivities."

"Almost, sir," said Bernie's father, quickly going over to shake his hand.

"Almost? *Almost?*" cried the owner. "Why, the Halloween parade has always meant a full house for the Bessledorf Hotel. What's wrong?"

"Well, it's a little matter of bats in the belfry, sir," said Theodore.

Lester crawled out from under the table, but Delores only glared at the intruder. "You almost gave me a heart attack, Mr. Fairchild," she complained.

"Lighten up, Delores!" Batman said jovially. "It's Halloween! Strange sights on the strangest of nights, you know! We are simply 'in the mood,' my dear, 'in the mood.' We will not let the Indiana Aztec stop the festivities. Isn't that right, Theodore?"

"Right as usual, sir," said Mr. Magruder. "All work and no play makes Jack a dull boy, eh, sir?"

Mr. Fairchild sat down at the table and helped himself to the family's dinner—a French fry off Bernie's plate, a pickle from Lester's, a radish from Delores. . . .

"Yes, yes, please do help yourself, Mr. Fairchild," Mother said quickly, hurrying to get an extra plate.

"Be our guest!" said Delores dryly. "Take the whole platter while you're at it."

Bernie was glad when it was time to go out trick-or-treating, because he didn't particularly want to sit and be polite to Mr. Fairchild, who was out in the lobby now, scaring the cats, alarming Mixed Blessing, and sending

109

Salt Water fluttering about the lobby squawking, "Time to go! Time to go! Awk! Awk!"

As soon as Georgene and Weasel came by in their costumes, Bernie set out with his friends.

"Why don't we take the left side of Bessledorf Street down as far as the church," Bernie suggested. "When we get to the Scuttlefoots' house, we'll sneak around in back and look for a grave."

"It's *dark* out, Bernie! How are we going to find a hump or a lump?" asked Georgene.

"Flashlight," Bernie told her, patting his pocket.

"And if Mr. Scuttlefoot *is* alive and comes out of his house to ask what we're doing in his backyard?" said Georgene.

"Then we'll tell him we're just checking out his flower bed," said Weasel. "Rescuing one of his cats. Taking a shortcut."

There were lots of ghosts and goblins out on the town. Grown-ups were dressed up too. The three friends had not gone a block before they ran into a man in a clown suit, a woman dressed as Mary Poppins, and a man in a Santa Claus costume. Even Clementine Carlson and Harold Higgins were out shaking hands with people on Halloween night, Clementine in a black wig and Harold with a fake nose and mustache.

As Bernie and his friends went from door to door, they got jelly beans from the bus depot, popcorn balls from the funeral parlor, chocolate bars and Gummi Bears, Milky Ways and lemon drops.

There was a light on downstairs in the Scuttlefoots' house, and Georgene didn't much like opening the huge iron gate.

"We'll just go around in back and see what we can find," Bernie instructed.

They walked single file around the house, and when they got to the garden, Bernie turned on his flashlight.

There was a concrete bench, a flower bed covered with leaves, an empty birdbath, a toolshed, a section of old fencing . . . There were flowerpots and trash cans, a garden hose, a rake, and a cat or two watching from the back steps.

"Even if somebody *was* buried here, Bernie, we'd never know it because everything is covered with leaves," Georgene told him.

"You're right," said Bernie disappointed. "We'd have to rake everything to see if the ground had been disturbed. I guess we'll have to come back in the daytime and find an excuse to check it out. Offer to rake or something."

"Shall we ring the doorbell and say 'trick or treat'?" Weasel asked.

"An old widower isn't going to have anything to give out on Halloween," said Georgene. "I'll bet he hasn't even gone to the store."

"Maybe he'll give out five-dollar bills if the Scuttlefoots were as rich as everyone says they were," said Weasel hopefully.

They walked around to the front of the house, still debating whether or not to go up to the door, when suddenly Weasel cried, "Look!"

They stopped in their tracks and looked where he was pointing.

In the narrow passage between the church and the Scuttlefoots' house, Santa Claus, in his fur-trimmed cap and boots, was swinging on a rope attached to the belfry, and was climbing up the side of the building.

Fifteen

THE GREAT TINTINNABULATION

"Flute Scoott! I'll bet it's him!" cried Bernie.

"Let's go get Officer Feeney!" said Georgene. "He can catch the guy in the act!"

"I saw Feeney outside the drugstore just a few minutes ago," Weasel said, and the three friends turned and began to run at top speed.

When they got there, they were so breathless they could hardly talk. Officer Feeney was standing outside the drugstore eating a sack of gumdrops when they rushed up and grabbed his arm.

"Santa Claus!" Bernie gasped.

"The belfry," panted Weasel.

"Flute Scoott!" wheezed Georgene.

"What in tarnation are you kids talkin' about?" asked Feeney.

There was no time to waste, Bernie knew. "The bats in the belfry," he said. "We know what they are and who's behind it. Somebody's up there! *Hurry*, Feeney!"

113

The policeman stuffed the gumdrops back in his pocket and began to run toward the church. "Why, I locked up the church myself, just so vandals couldn't get in on Halloween night," he puffed.

But just as they reached the great mahogany doors, they heard a loud resounding *clunk,* then a *clang,* then a series of frightful *bongs* and *dongs* and *bings* and *dings,* of clanging and banging and dinging and ringing— such a tintinnabulation of bells Bernie had never heard before, followed by shouts and bellows, more bangs and bongs, and suddenly everyone in town seemed to be running toward the church.

Bernie looked up and could hardly believe his eyes, for there in the belfry, bathed in a pale green light, was Santa Claus wrestling with old Mr. Scuttlefoot, who had a baseball bat in his hands and was trying to knock down the bells.

"That *song*!" shouted Mr. Scuttlefoot over the crowd below, taking another swing and bringing down another bell. "It's driving me crazy! I can't abide 'Abide with Me' one more minute! Day and night! Night and day! Every fifteen minutes, every hour on the hour!" He swung again, and another bell toppled.

And the man in the Santa suit kept saying, "Now, Dad. . . . Now, Dad. . . ."

"*Dad?*" exclaimed Bernie. "You mean Flute Scoott is really Scuttlefoot, Junior?"

"Why, his son must have come home!" said somebody else. "I heard that he argued with his parents years ago and said he'd never come back."

Everyone down below was watching the battle in the belfry, and Officer Feeney rushed inside the church.

"Why is old Scuttlefoot just now going bananas?" one man asked. "Those bells have been driving *us* nuts for a whole month!"

"Yeah, where's *he* been all this time that he doesn't know what we've been through!" said a woman.

Suddenly a third figure appeared in the belfry, that of Officer Feeney. With the help of the man in the Santa Claus suit, they were able to subdue old Mr. Scuttlefoot. At last the swinging stopped, the echo of the last bell died down, the green light went out, and a few minutes later, Officer Feeney and Santa Claus came out the front door of the church and took old Mr. Scuttlefoot into the house next door.

A mighty cheer from Harold Higgins's supporters went up when they realized that the bells were really silenced. Those who were going to vote for Clementine Carlson immediately began chanting, "Bring back the bells! Bring back the bells!" but they were drowned out by the cheering and jeering of the others.

Bernie, however, could hardly stand it. It was over! Officer Feeney had gone up in the belfry and must have seen what was up there. He would have figured it out in no time. Not only would the remote control have been discovered, but the bells were down, and Bernie hadn't had anything to do with either one, except to hand the case over to Officer Feeney.

"Bernie!" Georgene cried in dismay. "We lost out!"

"How could it have happened?" said Weasel.

"We should have taken our story to the newspaper first thing this morning instead of waiting for Halloween to be over," said Georgene.

"Now *none* of us will get our pictures in the paper!" said Weasel.

Bernie couldn't even speak, he felt so bad. None of them wanted to go on trick-or-treating after that. They headed back to the Bessledorf Hotel, their faces as long as yardsticks.

"Did you hear the news?" cried Mrs. Magruder as soon as she saw them. "Someone was up in the church belfry attacking the bells!"

"I was just coming back from the drugstore with my stomach medicine," old Mr. Lamkin said, "and I saw the whole thing. A lunatic was up there with a baseball bat!"

"Hallelujah!" cried Mrs. Buzzwell. "No more 'Abide with Me.'"

But Felicity Jones didn't seem happy at all about the attack on the bells and composed a poem on the spot:

"Oh, joyous bells in yonder sky,
That teased the ear and pleased the eye,
What foe did cut thy music short?
Thy playful ringing to abort?
Thy lovely sound shall be no more,
For far upon a distant shore . . ."

Delores interrupted:

". . . I clap my hands and nod my head
Because those bells are finally dead."

And when Felicity cast her mournful eyes about the room, Delores said, "Stifle it, Felicity. If I never hear 'Abide with Me' again, I'll be a happy woman."

Costumed children continued to enter the lobby for Mrs. Verona's chocolate cookies, but Bernic, Georgene, and Weasel sat glumly on the sofa, Mixed Blessing at their feet.

They didn't even count their gum balls or trade their chocolate bars. They didn't taste their caramel apples or chew their candy corn. Now Officer Feeney would tell his story to the newspaper, and it would be *his* picture that made the front page of the *Middleburg News* the next morning.

A half hour later the lobby doors swung open and in came the policeman, followed by a gaggle of reporters and photographers. Mixed Blessing howled, the cats hid, and Salt Water paced nervously back and forth on his perch, flapping his wings and squawking, "Man the lifeboats! Awk! Awk!"

"Mrs. Magruder," Officer Feeney called to Bernie's mother. "I have had quite an evenin', if I do say so myself, and I would like a cup of your delicious coffee and a piece of banana cream pie, if you don't mind."

"Oh, Officer Feeney, it's true, then! You *did* go up in the church belfry and catch the lunatic who was knocking down the bells."

"I did indeed, Mrs. Magruder. Seems that old Mr. Scuttlefoot couldn't even hear those bells all this time, nor 'Abide with Me' either, because he was so deaf. Too deaf to even answer his doorbell. Till this mornin', that is, when he got his first hearin' aid, and then he was hearin' all kinds of things he'd rather not hear a'tall."

He sat down at a little table in the lobby while Mrs. Verona brought him a piece of banana pie and a cup of coffee, and the photographers snapped away as he ate. The policeman went on:

"It seems that old Scuttlefoot couldn't stand for even one day what the rest of us folks here in Middleburg have been hearin' for the last month or so, and when he realized the noise would go on all night, he goes up to the belfry himself and tries to bring those bells down. A couple of 'em are broken, but I wager they can be fixed. If it wasn't for his son who helped wrestle that baseball bat out of his hands, no tellin' what he might have done."

"Son?" said Mrs. Magruder. "I didn't know he had a son."

"Oh, he's a grown man. Been livin' down in Miami, he tells me. He and his folks had words years ago, and he left Indiana, never to return, he said. Didn't even come back for his ma's funeral. But when he got wind of what was happenin' with the bells, and how—if they ever stopped ringin'—both he and his dad would be out their inheritance—he figured he'd better do somethin' about it. And right now he and his dad are havin' a nice cup of tea, and maybe that will calm the old man down and patch things up between 'em."

The reporters hung on every word, and flashbulbs popped as the photographers snapped more pictures. Bernie, Georgene, and Weasel moved in a little closer so they could hear what Officer Feeney had to say.

"How did Mr. Scuttlefoot get up there, Officer?" one of the reporters asked. "I understood that the church doors were locked tonight to keep out Halloween vandals."

Feeney nodded. "Oh, that son is a clever one," he said. "All the Scuttlefoots had a key to the belfry—the only folks who did. And old Mr. Scuttlefoot, being a deacon, had a key to the church door as well. But the son didn't. He knew that the church doors were unlocked most of the time, but in case they weren't, he had rigged himself a rope to the belfry should he ever need it, and kept it danglin' down the side of the building between the church and his dad's house. A good thing, too, 'cause if he hadn't got up there tonight, the damage would have been worse."

Now all the reporters were shouting out questions at once.

"A rope? But why did the son think he would need to get up there at all?"

"Why . . . uh . . . to keep an eye on those bells, I imagine . . ." said Officer Feeney, suddenly confused.

"But what about the bats?"

"Yes! The bats! Tell us about them, Officer Feeney!"

Now Officer Feeney looked very befuddled indeed. "Why . . . why . . . the bats . . . uh . . ."

"Can you tell us exactly what an Indiana Aztec bat looks like up close, seeing as how you were right up there in the belfry with them?" called out another reporter.

"Hmmm," the policeman said, frowning and placing his fork back on the table. "Well, now, it was dark up in that loft, except for the pale green light comin' from their nests, you know. But my first thought was not for my own safety but that of old Mr. Scuttlefoot, who never should have gone up there in the first place." And he nervously wiped his chin with his napkin.

"But Officer Feeney," said another reporter. "If Indiana Aztec bats have been nesting in the belfry, you certainly would have *seen* them. We all know that they are supposed to attack anyone who disturbs their nesting place. Did they attack you?"

Officer Feeney cleared his throat: "Oh, indeed they did!" he said. "But I swung *this* way and *that* way and *this* way and *that* way . . . and away they all flew, like the down of a thistle."

Everyone fell silent. The reporters looked at Feeney, then at each other.

"To tell the truth, I didn't get a really good look at them. . . ." Feeney said uncomfortably.

Bernie pushed his way through the reporters until he was standing right in front of Officer Feeney. "The reason you didn't see any Indiana Aztec bats, Officer Feeney, is because there aren't any," he said.

THE SPHC

Now all the reporters and photographers were staring at Bernie and his friends. It was perfectly clear to Bernie that in all the hullabaloo, Officer Feeney had not even thought to look for the bats once he was up there, so intent was he on stopping old Mr. Scuttlefoot. He was certainly braver than Bernie had ever been. But the policeman also didn't want to admit that he had missed his chance to observe an Indiana Aztec up close.

"Well, now, I *looked* for the bats, you can be sure," Feeney said. "Yes, indeed, I had my eye out for them, all right. But all I saw were . . . well, springs and sprongs and batteries and plastic flibbertigibbets and . . ."

"You were looking at springs and sprongs and batteries and plastic because *this* is what has been flying around the belfry at night," Bernie said. And he reached into his jacket pocket and pulled out the toy bat wing.

The reporters gasped.

"And here is their ghastly green light," added Weasel,

reaching into *his* pocket and holding up the green-painted lightbulb.

"And *we* think that Mr. Scuttlefoot's son, otherwise known as Flute Scoott, has been up in the belfry all these nights, flying those bats around by remote control," said Georgene. "He's probably the same one who put up those warnings all over town, trying to scare us into believing in those bats."

"Aha!" said Bernie's father. "He must have heard that if the bells ever stopped ringing, the town would have to give back all the gifts that Eleanor Scuttlefoot has given over the years, and the family fortune would go not to him and his father, but to the SPHC, otherwise known as the Society for the Protection of Homeless Cats."

"I see, I see!" said Mr. Fairchild, enjoying the detective story. He walked around the little table where Officer Feeney was sitting, picked up the policeman's fork, and took a bite of his banana cream pie without so much as a "Do you mind?"

"And to be sure that the bells would not be disconnected by someone who did not appreciate their music," Mrs. Magruder put in, "Eleanor made sure that the controls for the chimes were in the belfry itself, and only she and her family had the keys. Is that not right, Officer Feeney?"

"Right as rain," said the policeman, while the reporters scribbled away.

"Then it stands to reason," said Mr. Fairchild, "that with everyone getting more and more upset over that music at all hours of the day and night, somebody might get it in his head to climb up there and steal those bells or worse. So Scuttlefoot, Junior, thought up something so scary that no one would even *want* to go up in the belfry and try it." He turned to Bernie, Georgene, and Weasel. "And if it weren't for these three kids, the folks here in Middleburg might *still* be too frightened to climb up there and see what's what."

Officer Feeney was beginning to get the picture at last. "So if Scuttlefoot, Junior, could keep the public believin' in the Indiana Aztec bat until his elderly father died, bein' close to the age of ninety already, then it would be worth the trouble and the work it took him to go up there every night and send those bats flyin' around for a couple of hours."

"But you say the son lives in Miami," said a reporter. "Did no one see him around town?"

"He's been gone so long no one recognized him," said Feeney.

"But where has he been staying?" asked one of the photographers.

"In room 107, right here in this hotel," said Bernie, and heard his parents gasp. "He had a key to the belfry, like the rest of the family."

"But tonight, when the church doors were locked,

we saw him go up the side of the church in his Santa Claus suit," said Weasel. "He didn't know that his dad was on his way up the stairs inside with a baseball bat, I guess."

"I'll have to arrest that man for disturbin' the peace with them plastic bats, but I think I'll let him and his dad enjoy their tea first, and then we'll see what's what," Officer Feeney said. "I expect they've got a lot of catchin' up to do."

The reporters ran for the telephones to call in their stories.

"What a story! What a night!" said Mr. Lamkin. "Why, this was more exciting than the day Delores jumped out of an airplane."

"But what a sad ending for old Mr. Scuttlefoot and his son, for now that the bells are down, they will lose their fortune," said Mrs. Magruder. "No one will let them hook up those bells again. Not even Clementine Carlson will fight for that, for she would surely lose the election if she tried."

"But how did you know that the man in the Santa Claus suit—the man in room107—was Mr. Scuttlefoot's son, Bernie?" Theodore Magruder asked.

Bernie looked at Georgene. "Tell them," he said.

"Because he registered under the name of Flute Scoott, and if you rearrange the letters, it spells Scuttlefoot," explained Georgene.

"Doggone it, Bernie!" said Officer Feeney, exasperated. "Can't I just once solve a mystery all by myself without you and your friends gettin' in the act?"

Bernie grinned. "You ought to make us partners, Feeney. Georgene and Weasel, too."

There were more flashbulbs as the photographers took pictures. Georgene put one hand on her hip and turned slowly around, smiling in all directions.

But Felicity Jones was not reassured. "Please," she said, stepping forward. "What if those warning signs were *not* put there by Mr. Scuttlefoot's son at all? What if, indeed, there *is* a species called the Indiana Aztec, but it doesn't reside in the belfry?"

Now Joseph stepped forward waving a paper in his hand. "Because the veterinary college was visited today by the world's most renowned bat zoologist," he said. "I have it here in writing, signed and notarized, that there is not and never has been such a bat; it is simply a figment of an overactive imagination."

"But who was tailing old Mr. Scuttlefoot besides you, Officer Feeney?" asked Bernie. "I saw someone the night you escorted him home from our hotel. It wasn't just the old man's imagination."

"That I can answer," said Feeney, standing up and adjusting his jacket. "His son explained it to me. He was afraid someone might harm his father because of those danged bells, so he often followed him around at night just to make sure he got home safely when he was out and about."

Once again flashbulbs popped, cameras whirred, and the following day, there on the front page of the *Middleburg News* was the story of *The Bat Scam*, as it was called. On the inside, a double-page spread had photos of everyone involved, including Bernie and his friends.

Scuttlefoot, Junior, even allowed the photographer to take pictures of his fantastic six-piece remote-control deluxe super-quiet bat machine, that could keep six bats in the air at one time. And when the police searched his room at the Bessledorf Hotel, they found a bat repair kit, more bat warning posters, extra batteries and wires, and plastic flibbertigibbets. But because he cooperated fully, he was given a suspended sentence, plus one hundred hours of community service, the first hour being to go around town removing all the posters that had caused so much worry in Middleburg.

At school on Monday, the teacher asked Bernie and Georgene and Weasel to stand up in front of the class and tell the whole story from the beginning. And at dinner that evening, everyone was glad at the way things had turned out—everyone but Delores.

"You could have told us before, Bernie!" she wailed. "I might have had *my* picture in the paper too!"

"How's that?" asked Bernie.

"If I had known that the man in room 107 was going to inherit Eleanor Scuttlefoot's fortune, I would have been sweet to him from the start, no matter how big a slob he is, I would have said, 'Your wish is my command,' when he did not want to be disturbed, and perhaps those bells would have been ringing for us right now. We would have been married and it would have been *our* picture on the front page of the *Middleburg News*. As it is, all you can see of me in that picture is the end of my nose, one hand, and half a foot."

"Then let that be a lesson to you, my dear," said Theodore. "Money is the root of all evil, but half a foot is better than none. In the future, treat all guests graciously, prince and pauper alike, for who knows when a frog might be a prince in disguise."

"Huh?" said Lester. "What's he talking about, Bernie?"

"How to marry a millionaire, I think," Bernie told him.

As for the Scuttlefoots, Mr. Magruder then announced that he had attended a town council meeting that day, and it had been decided that the Scuttlefoot husband and son would get to keep their inheritance after all, and the town would not have to return the many gifts that Eleanor Scuttlefoot had given to Middleburg.

"The bells will be restored and assembled again, and go on playing 'Abide with Me' as before," he said.

And when the family howled in protest, he added, "However, Mrs. Scuttlefoot's will did not say just how *loudly* the bells must play, and so it has been agreed that their clappers will be wrapped in cotton batting, and they will play so softly that unless folks are standing right beside the church with their ears cupped to the wind, they will think that the faint music they hear is merely the breeze blowing through the poplar trees, and no one will be the wiser."

"Excellent, Theodore! How very clever!" exclaimed his wife.

"But what about homeless cats?" asked Bernie, looking at Lewis and Clark in one corner, whose bright green eyes, in turn, were boring through the family. *Yes,* they seemed to be saying. *What about the cats?* "They're the ones who lose out," Bernie said, "because if the bells stopped playing, all that money would have gone to them."

"Ah! We have taken care of that as well," said Theodore. "For the town council has passed a resolution that in memory of our dear departed Eleanor Scuttlefoot, every resident is urged, nay, *required,* to be kind to any hungry feline who happens to be passing through."

The whole family turned slowly around and studied Lewis and Clark as Theodore continued. "Every kitty, cat, and tomcat in need of a warm bed, a bowl of milk, or a sardine or two, is to be treated with affection, with the understanding that if the homeless cats of Middleburg are neglected, the flannel may be taken off the clappers, and the bells will once again ring out every quarter hour, and 'Abide with Me' will be our constant companion."

"Not a chance!" said Delores. "I'll be kind to a dozen cats before I go through *that* again!"

And Lewis and Clark, licking their paws by the stove, suddenly rose, stretched themselves, and strode royally out into the hotel lobby, their tails held high in the air.